DATE DUE

Nov29 '76			
GAYLORD			PRINTED IN U.S.A.

SEAPORTS IN THE MOON

SEAPORTS IN THE MOON

A Fantasia on Romantic Themes

By
VINCENT STARRETT

Garden City, New York
DOUBLEDAY, DORAN & COMPANY, INC.
1928

To
RAY LATIMER

TO THE DISMAYED PURCHASER

When I was a small boy in my grandfather's library, history, as I read it, without sense of time or causes, was in large part a confused and glamorous nightmare. I read it chiefly in romantic works of fiction, and, skipping the dates and the statesmen, read diligently the battles and the love-making. A great many years have gone over my head since those days, and although I still read history with some avidity, the glamour has largely departed and even the confusion is beginning to resolve itself. I regret the circumstance exceedingly; and so, in this parable of Man's quest for his vanished youth, I have endeavoured in some fashion to recapture both as once I felt them. At least, the outrageous chronicle is consecutive in its chronology, and some few of its episodes may even have been true, for all that anyone can say to the contrary. To those, however, who at some point in the perusal may feel their minds slipping, I can only say: be thankful that I did not involve General Winfield Scott in the fall of Granada and the Prince of Wales in the election frauds at Baltimore.

THE AUTHOR.

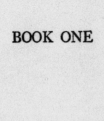

BOOK ONE

SEAPORTS IN THE MOON

CHAPTER ONE

IN WHICH TWO SCHOLARS MEET UPON THE SANDS

How or when he died, whether decently in bed or trussed up to a gallows, remains a riddle for foolhardy commentators.

—R. L. STEVENSON.

Old inhabitants can hardly fail to remember that excessively hot summer of the year 1483. It had been long in coming—after a rainy and miserable spring—but with its arrival other worries ceased. All over the known world the humidity was distressing. Depending upon their circumstances, citizens broiled in their homes or simmered at the seaside. The city merchants drooped in their counting houses. In Cordova, a member of the military police, bending over a public pool, was thrust into the water by the pressure from behind, and almost drowned by the weight of his armour before he could be rescued. The royal courts moved

frantically from place to place, attended by their
trains. A number of desultory wars were in
progress, but all languished by reason of the heat.
The arts moved but slowly. As the learned Floren-
tine, Toscanelli, said, and the best minds of Europe
agreed with him, seldom before in the history of
letters had perspiration and genius been so closely
allied. Fat monarchs are said to have wilted on
their thrones, and only half-jestingly to have
offered their daughters in marriage to any who
would avert complete dissolution. Butter melted
in the ice chest. Only crime and the church really
flourished. It was very hot.

In this pass, there were three camps that notably
stood forth in defense of their opinions. There were
those who contended that it was not the heat but
the humidity that bothered the world, those who
asserted that, in point of fact, many previous
summers had been hotter, and those who rather
alarmingly declared their belief that the seasons
were changing. Meanwhile, the extraordinary situation that had existed before the heat wave,
continued. In every city, village, and hamlet incredible scenes were reënacted, as the business of
life went forward. Lovers continued to wed in
haste and to repent at leisure, babes continued to
be born in and out of wedlock, men and women

continued to grow old reluctantly and reluctantly to die. Husbands toiled and wives scolded. Thieves broke in and stole. Scholars wrangled. Young bloods overslept in the morning and were late at the office. Children disobeyed their parents, and had stomachaches when they overate. Men borrowed money from their friends and were dunned by their landlords. Clocks were never on time. Fools cried for the moon, and cats littered in the kitchen. Sunday came immediately after Saturday. The price of mutton was a disgrace. On every hand, vice and virtue contended for supremacy, and heaven and hell were the alternatives of living. A bewildering predicament, and there were many who wondered what it was all about, and many who claimed to know. And there were also many who neither knew nor cared, as long as there was good wine to be drunk and a silver piece or two to jingle in the pocket. A memorable year. God slept in His heaven, all was wrong with the world. A remarkable year, quite unlikely to be forgotten. . . . All this is known. I recapitulate briefly for the sake of the record.

This, then, was the situation in Europe and the discovered islands of the sea, along toward evening of a trying day in the late summer of that depressing year, when an extraordinary adventure

befell a poor scholar, resident in Funchal, as he
walked the sands and looked out upon the water,
shifting now blue now green under the diminishing
light of the sun. He was a man somewhat above
middle height, strongly made, with red hair and
eyes the colour of the sea. While he did not particularly like the heat that had fallen upon the world
and Madeira, neither did he especially mind it, for
he was in his way a philosopher. He had been a
wool comber, then a sailor, and was now by profession a map maker. The anxieties of Europe
rested as lightly upon his shoulders as did his
threadbare cloak, for he had other matters than
either to think about. For one thing, he was nearing
forty now—a distressing circumstance—and no
longer an optimist about life and its rewards; and
for another, he held opinions so at variance with
the views of most other savants of his time, that
it behooved him to think well upon them, read
diligently, and be ready at all times to defend
them. He was quite penniless.

The sands at this point were deserted, and the
scholar walked slowly, in meditative fashion, as
his feet led him. Only that afternoon he had dis-
puted with the prior of the neighbouring convent
on the subject that was nearest to his heart. He
was simple enough, this poor scholar, to believe

that the earth, if not round like a ball, was at least pear-shaped and not flat like the top of a table; but the prior had remained unconvinced.

"Can anyone be so foolish," the ridiculous priest had asked, "as to believe that there are men whose feet are higher than their heads, or places where trees grow backward and rain falls upward? Where is the marvel of the hanging gardens at Babylon, if we are to allow a hanging world at the antipodes?"

"Pot-bellied fool!" muttered the philosopher, spurning a sand heap with his foot. "It is a pity there are no hanging gardens in Funchal, since there are so many here who deserve to hang. Or in Lisbon, for that matter! I can imagine a delightful picture. This idiot prior and His Christian Majesty of Portugal hanging sweetly together, like a pair of twins. They would look well by moonlight. . . . And if I reply that those who are opposite to *us* doubtless wonder that *we* do not fall, it is politely suggested that I am of unsound mind. Would God I were a few years younger and might find myself a patron! I would give them all something to raise their eyebrows over. Give me a single caravel, by God, with only twenty men— and I will show this old world as clean a pair of heels as ever twinkled over the horizon. . . . Yet

I suppose if I brought back the Grand Khan himself, under hatches, they would say I had picked
him out of the sea!"

He remembered his reception at the Portuguese
court, and the richly attired papal emissary with
whom he had conversed.

"Who are *you*, and what benefit do you bring
us?" that ecclesiast had cried. "What subtile discovery have *you* made? Tell us what revelation has
been made to *you*, that has been made to no one
else before you. . . . As for me, I listen to the prophets and the apostles. I obey the gospels. And
even if an angel should come from heaven to teach
us what was contrary to those laws, he should be
accursed."

"And yet, the time will come," mused the philosopher, striding the sands, "when all that I have
spoken will make me seem to have been a prophet.
So runs the world away! The heresies of to-day are
the commonplaces of to-morrow. It is a reflection
that does little to fill one's purse or stomach, however. Yes, some day they will know; and when
that day arrives, what will have become of me? A
memory for two or three old beldames—the rest
a roving dust upon the wind!"

He turned his bold blue eyes from the sea and
looked back for a moment at the sprawling town

on its declivity. The white convent, dwarfed by distance, sat smugly in its gardens of fruits and flowers. An ox sled was slowly climbing the steep road toward its gates. With a shrug of his broad shoulders, the sardonic scholar brought his glance back to the sea and resumed his stroll.

"One thing is certain," he concluded. "Another fortnight on this infernal island will about finish me. I swear that every day I feel my mind departing. I shall ship as a common sailor, if need be. Perhaps I shall have a try at France or England. The world may be small, but it can not be *quite* filled with fools."

Rounding a sharp headland that ran out into the ocean in such wise as to conceal what lay beyond, he came upon a little bay, and saw with surprise, labouring heavily in the tide, a small caravel that had drifted in from the sea. It wallowed awkwardly in the miniature harbour, now broadside on, now pitching headforemost toward the beach, at the mercy of the waves. It was almost upon the land when he came upon it, and in a short time its timbers struck and shivered. The vessel heeled over at the impact and lay half upon its side, its high poop well out of the water, in an attitude at once pathetic and ridiculous. Then, suddenly, as he advanced upon it, he saw a man stir upon its boards and stagger with descending steps toward the beach.

"By heaven!" cried the scholar, " 'tis a wreck!"

Pity for the unfortunate derelict stirred him. He hastened toward the spot at which the man would touch the land, and reached it in time to receive the drooping stranger in his arms. Then, observing that the man had fainted, he laid him on the sand and knelt beside him.

He was a small man, but of savage and sardonic mien, whiskered and moustachioed like a Frenchman. His cheeks were fallen in, and there were heavy troughs beneath his eyes. Obviously, this man was dying of hunger and thirst. Yet it seemed incredible that he should have voyaged far, alone . . . unless . . .

A thrilling and almost paralyzing thought came to the scholar, and for a moment shook him so that the sea and the land seemed to revolve in dizzying circles.

Cupping his hands, he carried water from the sea and hurriedly bathed the stranger's temples. In a little time, he was happy to see the man's eyes open. For a moment, they stared wildly, then settled upon those of the scholar, where they rested with an expression of fierce and questioning regard. The hollow voice spoke.

"Who are you?" it asked, like the croaking of a raven.

"A poor scholar, my friend," replied the rescuer, surprised by the inquiry. "By name Cristoforo Colombo. A native of Genoa. Now friendless and penniless in this land, much as yourself whom I have had the good fortune to succour. And you?"

A lean arm curved upward and caught him by the shoulder.

"A scholar!" cried the stranger, harshly. "Did you say a *scholar*? Then I am fortunate indeed. Great God, what fortune!"

For a moment, he lay back upon the sand, as if summoning his strength, then swiftly twisted himself so that he lay upon his side and elbow. "Listen, my friend," he continued, with strange triumph. "I see pity in your eyes. You are planning to save my life; to carry me on your back, perhaps, and bring me to food and water. Do not waste your time or mine. At the end of your journey you would find only a corpse across your shoulders. I am dying, and you cannot save me. I cannot save myself. But before I go, I can whisper my secret in your ear. The secret that only I possess—the secret of eternal youth!

"Listen, you fool!" he cried fiercely, as the other's eyebrows lifted. "If you are a scholar, listen! I am not raving. Has it occurred to you, ever, in your dreams between sleep and sleep, that there are great new lands beyond this sullen waste of waters?"

For an instant, he glared ferociously into the eyes of the Genoese; then, at the scholar's start of understanding, a gleam of satisfaction lighted the haggard face.

"I see that it is so," continued the dying man more quietly. "You have dreamed it as all scholars worthy the name have dreamed it. It is my great fortune to have found you, here at the end of my life. It revives one's faith in God, even as did the lands beyond the sea. Your hand, my friend, within mine, a poor scholar of Paris. Many months ago, I sailed with fifteen others upon that caravel, which now has tossed me at your feet. We were returning with a great secret when illness struck us down, a strange malady of which all died but me. We had found another world, a world of such rare delights that I would have to live a year to catalogue them; a world of savage islanders and miraculous birds and flowers. Islands of enchantment—and in the midst of one of them, a running spring whose water is of such virtue as to make old men young and young men younger. A fountain of perpetual youth, in an island of such natural luxuries as to

make the mouthings of a priest about paradise a
child's prattle by comparison. Youth—life—and
love! And copper maidens of such voluptuous
symmetry——"

He interrupted himself in mid-flight. "Do I begin to interest you, my friend?" he smiled. "Or
do copper women interest you less than beaten
gold?"

"My experience of both," answered the scholar,
with some embarrassment, "has been limited. I
am afraid my thoughts have run, these several
years, on other matters."

"The more fool you!" retorted the dying man.
"What is it that you crave? What is your flaming
dream, that gold and women find no place in it?
Youth? Fame? I offer both—and gold and women,
too, for such as want them. Your hair is graying at
the temples, Scholar, as was mine. Look to it
that it does not go entirely. Accept the miracle I
offer you, or go your own way to the devil. Youth
is the touchstone of all happiness—and it was
youth we sought, youth that we all but found.
In France, there was a price upon my head; a
gallows yearned for me on Paris hill. Have you
ever been close to death upon the tree, Scholar?
There are pleasanter ways to die. It is not sweet
with nimble feet to dance upon the air! Twice I

have felt the hangman's hand upon my throat. He has a brutal thumb, the executioner of Paris. To-day, I perish warmly on the sands, my hand in his who will accept my gift of life. . . . Do not speak, my friend: listen! I have only a few moments left to live. It is there beyond the seas, the fountain of eternal youth. In an island the name of which is called by the natives Bimini. To you I bequeath the torch and the quest. Seek well! You will know it by the fountain. It is your secret now; I give it gladly. Look to it that you use it wisely. It is not for all who clamour for it. By my death, you shall live forever. By this, I shall atone——"

His arm sank beneath him. He fell back upon the sand, his eyes wide and terrible. The first scholar leaned quickly forward and raised the fallen head.

"I understand," he gasped. "What else? What more?"

"That is—all," whispered the dying stranger. "The secret—is now—with you. I trust——"

"And you?" cried Colombo, with feverish lips. "Your friends—your family—your name? Can I do nothing for you?"

"No friends," murmured the dying man, "no family. I, François Villon, a poor student of Paris.

A poor poet, m'sieu', by God's mercy and by your leave. . . ."

At this moment, death overtook him.

The remaining scholar rose upright and turned his eyes across the water. For a long time he looked seaward to the horizon, with unseeing eyes. In Portugal, the apes and asses still reigned and flourished. In France and England, things were little better. In Spain, their Christian majesties waged holy warfare with the Moors. What then?

With sudden decision, he turned his back upon the body and strode rapidly away toward the settlement, kicking the sand in gusts before him as he progressed.

When he had passed some five minutes beyond view, there came slouching along the beach from the other way a man of furtive demeanour and sidelong eyes, who stopped at sight of the corpse. After a moment, the newcomer glanced quickly about him, then stooped to the dead man's jerkin. But his exploring fingers drew forth only a small roll of parchment. Cursing the stranger's poverty, the man scrambled to his feet and for some minutes stood looking at the sorry plunder he had resurrected.

For the most part, the parchment sheets contained only writing, and that in a foreign language, but by the length of its lines the vagabond was able to guess that it was poetry. Upon one sheet, however, had been traced a rude map, and this he studied with greater care, for he had been a sailor and knew somewhat of the world. Apparently, it recorded the outline of a small island, but the writings in the margins he was unable to read.

For an instant, he wavered in indecision; then, with another oath, he tossed the roll of verse into the sea, and cramming the map into his pocket, turned back in the direction from which he had come.

When the tide had reached its height and ebbed again, there was none upon the sands to note that it had taken with it the body of François Villon.

CHAPTER TWO

IN WHICH A QUEEN FEARS THAT SHE IS
GROWING OLD

Meanwhile the Lord Chamberlain, with a piece of elastic, stood in a chair killing the little green flies that slept on the wall near the candle-sconces. "Whatever you three decide," he called to the others.
—PATRICK SCARLET.

In the privacy of the royal pavilion, a number of years later, a famous queen who had been attentively studying her reflection in a mirror put down the glass with a frown. For some moments, she sat and pouted thoughtfully at the rich hangings of the tent. At length she turned to her maid.

"There is not the slightest doubt about it," she observed. "I am becoming disgustingly fat. Before long, my eyes will be lost in rolls of tissue and I shall not be able to see myself, which will be a comfort. They say that after forty, it comes, and there is no hope. It comes, and that ends it. But I am certainly not forty yet, whatever I may look. One would think that this camp life would help to keep one's flesh within reasonable bounds."

The little maid raised a pair of horrified palms. "Your Majesty!" she panted.

"Don't tell me again that I never looked younger or more beautiful," said the Queen. "I hear it on all sides. It is what convinces me that I must be growing old."

She sighed deeply, and at the same instant a lady-in-waiting put her handsome head in at the door to say that the King's Majesty was outside. The Queen nodded.

"Say to His Majesty that I shall join him in just a minute," she answered. "The spectacle can wait. *I* am the greatest spectacle in camp, just now, I think. It is really abominable."

For several minutes, she bustled about, doing nothing in particular, and then, with a final disapproving glance at the mirror, stepped forth to join her husband. An aide sprang to her stirrup, and, in a moment, amid a flourish of trumpets, the royal party moved off. The procession thundered through the streets of the camp and out on to the plain. In a short time, it had reached the scene of the impending spectacle.

A giant catapult had been erected outside the walls of Granada. Its great springboard had been drawn back until the stout timbers groaned. On all sides, save immediately in front of the formidable engine, was gathered the chivalry of Spain. Near at hand stood a sturdy rascal with a mallet, and to the end of the plank two other ruffians were lightly tying the body of a man, whose legs and arms were folded and bound in such fashion that he resembled a large and irregular ball. Their Majesties surveyed the preparations with approval and stood back to await the outcome.

An order was given, and the clustering workmen fell away. The mallet swung sharply against the withholding cog. With a whir and crash, the curved board sprang up and outward, and the bound man shot away from its tip at incredible speed. He travelled with such velocity that he revolved only twice within view of the spectators before in a great curve he had vanished beyond vision.

A shout of satisfaction went up from the assembled throng, and in a few moments a yell of rage came back from the walls of the beleaguered city. Whereupon, purses of gold were distributed among the skilful labourers who had operated the engine, and the concourse began to disperse.

"An admirable shot," observed the King of Spain. "By now, I trust, he spatters the steps of the Alhambra. It will teach him caution, and his superiors—I hope—discretion. What think you of our marksmanship, my dear?"

The Queen shook her head with a doubtful smile. "For your marksmanship, Ferdinand," she replied, "I have only praise. As to your judgment, I am less sure. I should have thought a less dramatic and conspicuous death sufficient for the scoundrel. As matters stand, I fear that you have invited reprisals of a similar nature. I shudder to think what would occur to me, now, if I were to fall into the hands of the enemy."

The King shrugged. "It is a lesson these infidels have needed," he said. "It may suggest to them that spies are not welcome in our camp."

Isabella, however, had been right. An hour later, the body of a Galician gentleman, whom the Moors had promptly slain and set astride upon a mule, rode into the Christian camp and gave point to Her Majesty's apprehensions. Thereafter, her judgment was held by her husband in higher regard.

As it happened, another mule, almost at the same moment, was carrying another rider toward the same objective, but from another direction. But whereas one rider had brought death into the camp, the second was bringing a vigorous life— indeed, perennial life, he reflected, had his benefactors but the wit to underwrite him. As he rode, he gazed discontentedly at the panorama unrolled before him.

On all sides, the Spanish lines stretched away in thoroughfares of shifting colour. Lances glittered in the sun, and music ran lightly on the pleasant breeze. A confusion of plume and scarf and banner merged their hues—purple and scarlet, green and orange—into a motley flame that tongued and twisted above the activities of the soldiery. Had it not been for the occasional crashing of ordnance, one might have supposed a fair or kirmess to be going forward; even a coronation. Right and left stretched the gay tents of the besiegers, set off with flaunting pennons, save only in the great cleared space wherein a city of stone and mortar was being builded. Ahead, the battering machines banged and rattled and occasionally burst. In the intervals of cannonading, horses screamed and pranced, and the lively trumpets sent their bright ardours echoing across the vega and down the valleys.

Although the occasion was one of bloodshed, the opportunities for tournament and festival had not been neglected. Daily, on the level arena that stretched between the Christian camp and the beleaguered city, combats took place between the high mettled cavaliers of the opposing armies. Moslem heroes rode insolently forth from the city with reckless challenges, and truculent Spanish bravos paraded the arena, spoiling for a fight.

But to the middle-aged mariner riding into the picture from the convent of La Rabida, the spectacle meant no more than to the gray mule that he bestrode. He was tired of camps and sieges, tired of courts and monarchs, tired even of being tired. At the moment, he was particularly tired of mules, for his proper position was with legs braced upon a rocking deck, and he had come a long distance to snap his fingers at the Queen of Spain.

Peddling a new world from door to door, thought this excellent fellow, had proved a more discouraging enterprise than he had imagined. It had proved, in fact, a wearisome and thankless business. There would have been nothing to be surprised at if his enthusiasm had been measurably dampened when, after eight years of endeavour, he still found himself crying his wares in the market-place. A great many times he told himself that he would have shrewd need of those rejuvenating waters when he reached them. His patience, he informed himself, was nearing an end.

Recognizing the graying scholar, as he rode through their lines, some of the soldiers laughed and tapped their foreheads.

"It is Colon," they chuckled, "he who was Cristoforo Colombo. He would sail westward to reach the Indies. It is said that he believes God has no beard. He is madder than that fellow in Seville who swore that his mother was a man. What ho, Cristobal," they called, "what shape is the earth to-day?"

The victim of these pleasantries smiled down upon them with engaging malice.

"Gentlemen," he said, "I am in need of volunteers for a voyage to the moon. I propose to go there upon a gray mule furnished by the pope. It has been especially blessed for the journey. God save the Devil!" And he rode on, leaving them staring.

Yet, before he was out of hearing, his ears were burning, as he heard the words of the ribald ballad they hurled after him:

> "He swore the world was round-o,
> That land it could be found-o,
> That captivating, fascinating,
> Son of a bum, Colombo!"

On the last syllable of his name, the voices of the singers dropped to great depths, and it rolled forth like the boom of a buoy.

It annoyed him a great deal, as a great many things had annoyed him during the eight years that he had trailed the court from capital to capital. Had it not been for the Queen—whom God save— he would have thrown the whole enterprise over- board long ago. Or *would* he? There was no doubt, however, that her continued existence had made it all less difficult. She was a wonderful woman, and if she had had her way, he would have had his caravels before this. A remarkable woman, noble, virtuous, and tender. Not that there could ever be anything between them! Good God! she was like some remote and inaccessible star, brilliant and cold, yet beautiful as all the stars together.

One secret he had kept from her at their confer- ences: the secret of the perpetual fountain. That was still his own. It would be his own until the day when he could kneel before her, his heart upon his lips, offering her the precious drops as his ulti- mate gift—more precious even than all the islands of the sea. Who would might have the islands, since all kings must come at last to dust, but the fountain and its secret should be his own, forever; its miracle for such as he elected to make deathless.

At the door of the royal pavilion, he drew rein and painfully dismounted. A young knight, un- casqued and smiling, detached himself from a group of court ladies, at ease beneath a canopy, and approached. He was a member of the Queen's household, and known to the mariner by sight: a friendly youth with a talent for conversation and roguish adventure.

"You were not expected so soon, Excellency," said this officer. "Their Majesties have but this moment left for the arena, where a jousting is going forward. If you will condescend to wait, in good time they shall be notified of your arrival."

"Thank you," responded the mariner, "I shall with your permission notify them myself. . . . Do these ruffians give no indication of a desire to surrender?" he added, with a querulous gesture toward the distant walls.

"None," said the soldier. "They are as obdurate as Your Excellency's self."

"Then, by Saint James, they are upon the point of yielding," growled the other, remounting his placid animal, "for upon my word, young friend, I am about ready to raise my own siege."

"I trust you are not as badly off as they," smiled the knight affably. "Their magazines of grain are emptied, and for some weeks, we understand, they have been compelled to devour the flesh of horses and of dogs. Even the boiled hides of those animals are said to be a delicacy. In default of other nutriment, they make a salad of vine leaves, dressed in oil."

"How do you know all this?"

"From their deserters, who come to us daily to barter liberty for bread. Yesterday, one proved to be a spy. This morning, he departed quickly and in haste. An engine dropped him over the walls as neatly as if he were a pellet of marble."

"No doubt I shall be dispatched in some such fashion to the Indies," said the mariner sardonically. "I had as lief that as continue on as chief muleteer."

He clucked his tongue at the gray mule and jogged away through the camp to the tilting ground, toward which, from every hand, the soldiery was streaming.

A vast activity was evident in the neighbourhood of the arena as he approached, a wide and level stretch of ground lying midway between the city and the camp. In the centre of a deep circle of troops, with here and there the flutter of a woman's headdress, Colon beheld the united standards of Castile and Aragon, high above the surrounding banners. Toward this spot he directed his animal, and dismounting at the outskirts of the horde, pushed through until he was within sight of the spectacle.

The guns had fallen silent, and in the distance

he could see a cloud of Moorish warriors hovering
on the horizon of the tilting ground. In the centre
of the arena, their paladin, splendidly accoutred
and mounted, was cavorting with insolent bravado.
He was a gigantic figure, set high upon a gigantic
horse, and in the sunlight, as he rode toward the
Spanish lines, his great beard seemed blue and his
white teeth gleamed wickedly through his whiskered lips. Already, it appeared, this champion had
slain a pair of Spaniards, and the soldiers were
clamouring for his death.

In a moment, there was a flourish of trumpets,
and the Spanish champion appeared, riding slowly
toward the improvised lists. Then his lance dipped
in salute, and putting spurs to his horse he rushed
like a whirlwind upon the grinning Moor, who rode
with equal haste to meet him. The collision,
thought Colon, was like a meeting of planets.
Both men were instantly unhorsed and rolled
heavily in the dust, which coiled in spiral towers
around them. As they scrambled to their feet, with
flashing blades, the superior height of the infidel
behemoth was even more apparent. The Spaniard,
who was not a small man, seemed almost a dwarf
by comparison. Yet even as the Moor whirled up
his scimitar and sprang forward, the lighter Spaniard was in and out under the huge arms, like a

cat, and the earth seemed to tremble as the vast heathen bulk crashed forward.

For an instant, the Christian knight stood back, leaning idly upon his sword; then stepping to the corpse, he turned it upon its back, and suddenly stooping, slashed off the handsome beard.

A terrific shout went up from the Spanish arms. "Juan Ponce! Juan Ponce!" bawled the soldiers; and a shriek of anger answered from the hovering host of the enemy, who drew off without further challenge.

Colon, swept backward by the returning rabble, sought vainly to reach the royal standards, but the pressure was too great. He gave over the effort and with a shrug went in search of his mule, which he found cropping the short grass where he had left it. As he rode slowly back to camp, chance threw across his path the knight whose recent triumph over the Moorish champion had made him for the moment a favourite. Juan Ponce de León was riding gaily toward his own quarter of the field, with a knot of admiring officers around him. The Queen's gift of a golden chain glittered against his dusty cuirass, and the mariner saw it with a little pang of envy.

"That was well done, Juan Ponce," called the seaman. "You are very quick and sure."

Shrugging modestly, the other smiled back. "It was nothing," he deprecated. "You would have done as well yourself. But, hullo," he added suddenly, "it's Colon, isn't it? Colon the dreamer! What brings our famous scholar to the front?"

"Dreams!" answered the dreamer ironically. "Those very dreams you speak of. Her Majesty is good enough to wish to hear them again. I have been summoned for another conference; the forty-fourth, I think. If I am successful, perhaps I shall offer you a commission."

"By the mass, friend Cristobal," retorted the soldier, reining in his horse, "you might go farther and fare worse. I am beginning to tire of civilization. It cramps my talents. Give me a chance, and perhaps I shall not disappoint you."

"I shall write you down as my first volunteer," answered the mariner, and he rode on with a puzzled frown upon his brow. "Something has happened to make me popular," he muttered. "A little while ago, that lewd young cub with the hussies addressed me as Excellency. Now Ponce de León would sail with me. There must be rumours in the air. Has good Father Perez been successful, after all? Has the Queen at length decided to risk a venture?"

As he rode still farther upon his way, his suspicions were confirmed. A voice called to him from the camp's edge, and striding to his side came the young gallant about whom he had just been thinking. The boy laid a hand upon the bridle rein, smiling.

"What will you trade for good news, Excellency?" he asked. "The story has it that all has been arranged. You are to have your caravels and sail wherever you have a mind to go."

For an instant the mariner's pulses leaped. Then, "A likely story," he scoffed. "Where did you come by it, young gossip? Or have I yourself to thank for changing Her Majesty's mind?"

"More likely your friend the priest from La Rabida," answered the officer. "Yesterday he was in conference with Their Majesties for half an hour. To-day he has been at it again. It was by his insistence that you were summoned here. I think he has more power with the Queen than has the King. He was her confessor before he retired and Talavera came. It is a most important and confidential post. I suspect, Excellency, that you are in luck. Bring me a little ingot from the Indies, or the horn of an unicorn, if you can persuade one to spare it. Verily, I have need of both."

The mariner smiled grimly and shook his grizzled locks. "The ingot I can understand," he said. "I have need of ingots, myself. But why the horn, young ruffian? Is it your intention to establish a museum?"

"And you a scholar!" cried the other reproachfully. "Don't you know that in the olden times when an unicorn was to be captured, it was accomplished by the connivance of a virgin? 'Tis in all the books. What, then? I am in straits about a virgin, and possibly 'twill work the other way."

"Be off with you," cried Colon, with simulated indignation. "But stay! If it is new faces that you crave, you had better sign up to come along with me."

"Not I," chuckled the other. "I am in favour of the certainties. Just now they lead me on another quest. Besides, I said nothing about new faces."

He waved his hand joyously and swaggered away, leaving the mariner to his thoughts. For a moment, Colon sat motionless; then, pricking his animal with the spurs, he cantered rapidly along the road that led to the royal pavilions.

"It is true!" he cried. "By Saint James, it is true! Good Father Perez has turned the trick, and I am Admiral of the Ocean Sea! Give me but youth, now, and the world is mine!"

Once more he spurred the gray mule onward, and so came at length into the royal presence.

Kneeling with bared head before the Queen of Spain, Colon received the tidings of his triumph. They were alone together, save for the guards outside the doors of the pavilion and some ladies at a discreet distance. The Queen's eyes seemed heavy and there were lines at the corners of her eyes and mouth. She had aged perceptibly in the years that had passed since the mariner from Genoa first had sued her interest and protection. Her famous Spanish beauty was fading. She was growing stout. And yet, she could be no more than forty. A strong woman, a tall and handsome woman; but growing stout. A noble and virtuous woman; but growing stout. In her suit of armour, beside her leaner husband, she had seemed to dwarf him as they had stood together a little time before.

As if she read the thoughts that were passing in his mind, the Queen frowned.

"Colon," she said, "why do you stare at me so rudely? Is my face so plain? Does it occur to you, perhaps, that your queen is growing old?"

He seized her hand with an impulsive gesture and carried it to his lips.

"To the contrary, Majesty," he returned, "I

was thinking, since you ask, that never had I seen Your Majesty look so young."

"You are becoming quite a courtier, Colon," purred the Queen. "And yet, sometimes my mirror seems to say otherwise. Perhaps it is just that I am tired. . . . Know then that we have been pleased to acquiesce in your demands. To-morrow you shall have your official notice; your caravels as soon as I can pawn my jewels. Your prior from La Rabida, Colon, has been most eloquent in your behalf. He has pictured for us the realms of Mangi and Cathay even more ably than yourself could have portrayed them. . . . And yet, the wealth and splendour that he has painted are as nothing beside the urge of those higher principles which we hold sacred. It is our belief, as it is our desire, that the empire of the Cross should be extended over those benighted heathen whom you are to seek. Is that not, also, your own desire, good Colon?"

"Most certainly, Majesty. From the first, as I have often said, it has been my purpose to bring the blessed sacrament to those misguided mortals. I have no other thought."

Deeply affected, the Queen bent forward and lightly touched his sleeve.

"Colon," she murmured, "why have you told me nothing of those springs of youth?"

For an instant, the mariner was stricken dumb. In what mad moment of confidence had he told Perez that secret? No longer was there any wonder that the prior of La Rabida had been successful in his mission.

"Springs of youth?" he echoed, as if surprised.

"They bubble in an isle called Bimini. Until your Father Perez spoke of them, I had not dreamed of their existence."

Rising upright upon his feet, the admiral bowed deeply.

"Your pardon, Majesty," he said, with great humility. "I had not supposed that anyone so lovely as Your Majesty could be interested in what may be, at best, only a pretty fable. For myself, it had not occurred to me to credit the story."

She fanned his cheek gently with the cluster of feathers she carried in her hand and hummed a little tune.

"Still," said Her Majesty of Spain, "I think it would be as well to look into the legend, Colon, while you are in the neighbourhood. Say nothing to the King of this, but make what inquiry you think advisable, since, if this Bimini exists, 'twere well to add it to our standard."

She blushed and dimpled very prettily as she extended her hand for his kiss.

"And do not fail, Colon," she added, "to bring me back a vial of the waters. If I am not ugly yet, some day, no doubt, I shall be. One never knows! One never knows!"

CHAPTER THREE

IN WHICH A LEAN KNIGHT RIDES FORTH UPON
A QUEST

If you say to me, Master, it would seem that you were not very wise in writing to us these flimflam stories and pleasant fooleries; I answer you, that you are not much wiser to spend your time in reading them.
—FRANÇOIS RABELAIS.

All of which having occurred very much as I have related, some four to forty months thereafter there occurred two further matters of interest to our history. For the first, the caravels of Colon in due time sailed westward on their voyage, passing en route a fleet of vessels of the State bound outward for Africa with all the Jews of Huelva, a province in which these people were held in no great esteem. And for the second, an elderly gentleman, somewhat mad but no Jew, escaped the vigilance of his niece and his housekeeper, in a village of the Mancha, and rode forth upon an ancient steed, questing adventure. By your leave, we shall follow the fortunes of the latter.

Accompanied by his squire, when night had

fallen some hours, he rode earnestly toward the
fields of Montiel. And since both master and man
were eager to discourage pursuit, they rode rapidly
and under cover of darkness. Arrayed in a patch-
work armour, scrupulously polished and glinting
in the moonlight, the adventurer sat high upon his
rawboned horse, with his helmet before him on his
saddlebow. From time to time, as they progressed,
he laid a long finger perpendicularly alongside his
nose, and seemed to think profoundly. On the
church records of his district, this gentleman's
name was entered as Alonzo Quixada, but he himself preferred to be called Don Quixote, by which
name he was widely known and avoided. In
appearance, he was lean and gaunt, with a loose
mouth and a melancholy eye.

His squire, a short and comfortable citizen, famous for his common sense, was in all ways his
master's antipode. Mounted upon a good mule, he
ambled amiably at the heels of the horse Rozinante,
with little amorous glances at the lights that
glimmered here and there in the darkness, behind which, no doubt, attractive women were
disrobing.

"An admirable night for an adventure," observed the elderly gentleman, after a time, with
critical approval. "My only hope is that it may

not assail us from the rear. Ride forward, Sancho,
that we may talk together. I trust that my two
gossips, the curate and the barber, do not think to
visit me too early in the morning. I have no mind
to be the object of a hue and cry."

His companion shrugged. "Let them hue and
let them cry," said he. "Much good it may do
them! More likely they will wish us godspeed and
good riddance."

"Yet it is not they, exactly, that I fear," continued the knight. "They would but carry the
tidings of my departure to my niece; it is she who
would leave no stone unturned to apprehend me.
It is a curious circumstance, Friend Sancho, that
at no age does a man seem to be trusted by his
womenfolk. Thank God, I have no wife! That
humiliation at least has been spared me."

"In that, good sir, you speak truth," nodded the
squire, with admiration. "Their tongues are never
still. Clackety-clack, they are at it from dark
until daylight. They are like magistrates determined upon a conviction. To obey all of their be-
hests, one would have need to compress a lifetime
into every week. Believe me, I know what I am
talking about, since mine is a composite of them
all. Ho-ho! but what a sight it would be to behold
her in the morning, crying 'Sancho' here and

'Sancho' there—and Sancho on his way!" He rolled merrily in his saddle and chuckled aloud.

But the knight shook his head with sad disapproval. "I fear me, Sancho," said he contrarily, "that your sentiments do you no great credit. After all, is it not these creatures' affection for us that engenders their distrust? Yes, I am afraid you do not entertain those qualms and scruples that proverbially should assail one upon parting from his beloved. With my niece, now, it is different. Assuming all the masteries of a wife, she is lacking in all the tendernesses. It may be that I have over-persuaded you with my tales of faëry islands, and that we shall both be diligently pursued."

"Pursuit," observed Sancho Panza wisely, "is better than possession. Let them pursue us, good sir. I care not three skips of a louse." As he spoke, he turned nervously in his saddle and stared deeply into the retreating shadows.

"So be it," responded his master. "And since you do not regret, be sure that you shall not suffer by the adventure. I have promised you high preferments, and these you shall have, or I am unworthy the name of knight. In me are revived the glories of a decaying chivalry. Faugh! that the world has come to this. One used to see tournaments and armed men. Now it is thought a credit-

able thing to steal sheep and oxen." He snorted
with disgust.

"It is true," agreed the squire. "Since the passing of the Moor, a lamentable peace has fallen
upon the world. And yet, I like it very well," he
admitted. "Were it not for my island, I vow I
should not set forth upon this venture. I pray you
have a care, Sir Knight, that my island be not forgotten. Were it never so great, be sure that I
should be able to govern it."

Embracing his buckler, the lean knight shook
his lance so that it caught the glimmer of the stars.
"Islands are won as easily as straws are lifted,"
said he. "Be at ease, my friend. Have I not told
you that it was a custom very much used by ancient knights-errant, to make their squires the
governors of such islands and such kingdoms as
they conquered? It is a good custom, and I am
resolved not to abolish it. Within six days, it is
possible that you shall have come into your
kingdom."

"Ha!" cried Sancho Panza, with a deep breath;
and he rolled his tongue across his lips as if he had
been promised a glacé. "And would my wife Joan
become a queen, good sir, and all my children
princes?"

"Who can doubt it?"

"That can I," chuckled Sancho, "for I swear that if God in heaven rained kingly crowns upon the earth, with a kingdom under each, not one would sit with grace upon the head of that same Joan."

"Well, well," said Don Quixote, "you shall make of her what you please. When you are a king, the matter is easily arranged."

"I shall make her a countess," decided Sancho, as if he were conceding a point, "and let her sit beside a tollgate. The title will mean nothing to her, but the pennies will make her happy."

In this fashion, conversing pleasantly, they rode through the night, and at daybreak came upon the ancient fields of Montiel, where once upon another quest the knight had done battle with a windmill. Presently, signs of life began to appear. A flock of gaunt and threadbare sheep paraded across the road and disappeared into a hollow of the empty land. They were followed at no great distance by a brown and spare old shepherd, with white neglected hair falling over a tattered cloak, and on his face a smile of imbecile content. Close at hand, on the edge of the highway, stood an inn, above the porch of which hung a battered sign, and toward this crept a shrivelled old parrot of a woman, burdened with an earthen jar of water. At this hint of refreshment, the tired animals bestridden by the adventurers pricked up their ears and made all haste toward the place. The proprietor of the inn was taking down his shutters as they rode up.

"God save you, Sir Knight," said he, with great deference; and removing his cap to the apparition, he added: "In what fashion may I serve your honour?"

"With wine and bread, constable," replied the knight errant, "and food and water for our beasts. And, while I think of it, can you tell me whether there is anywhere about a damsel in distress?"

"A damsel in distress?" echoed the innkeeper, perplexed. "Indeed, I fear that you have been misdirected. In all the neighbourhood, there is not a dam——"

"Tut, tut," interrupted the knight testily. "A giant then, a dragon, or even an enchanted princeling who has been changed by magic into an innkeeper. It is our first adventure, and we are not particular."

But it appeared that the neighbourhood was in fact no better equipped for gallantry than the innkeeper would have said. As for an island to be conquered, he took oath that there was none within an hundred miles. In the end, the adventurers

were forced to content themselves with such food
and drink as they had requested. A table was set
for them in the inn door, and while their animals
munched in the stable, master and man fared very
well upon black bread and wine. Since neither was
accustomed to anything better, it was considered
very good provender indeed.

"None the less," said the knight of La Mancha,
draining his mug, "it is a great pity that there is
no damsel about, in whose defense I might break
a lance. Look yonder, Sancho, upon the female
who has just presented her eyes for our inspection.
Do you not fancy a resemblance there to the lost
princess of Brittany?"

"For all of me, good sir," replied Sancho, after
a rapid glance, "the lady may remain undiscovered until the crack of doom. She has an ankle like
my Uncle Blanco, who is a sufferer from the
gout."

"For shame, Sancho!" cried his master. "I have
no doubt that this is a most excellent and admirable woman, who is in no wise to blame for her
ankles. Nor was it upon her ankles that I looked;
although I grant you that they are perhaps not all
that one would seek in a princess of Brittany . . .
but, kind Heaven! what is it that the woman is
doing? Has she gone suddenly mad?"

The innkeeper's wife, as they were speaking, had turned quietly to her tasks, and was now engaged upon the wrapping of small sweets, or dulces as they were called, in little squares of paper.

"There is no madness in working before the heat sets in," observed the squire, without emotion. "Doubtless it is her morning chore, before the arrival of customers."

"She is destroying an immortal book!" cried the knight. "See how with every movement of her hand she tears away a leaf of the volume. Sweet Virgin! it may be the deathless *Amadis of Gaul*, itself. It is a sacrilege. Upon my knightly honour, I cannot permit it."

He leaped violently to his feet, so that his armour clattered with great din about him, and advanced upon the offending shopkeeper.

"Hold, woman!" he exclaimed, with upraised hand. "What is this volume that you destroy so ruthlessly? Are you possessed of all the wisdom of the world that you dare thus to demolish one single chapter of it?"

The dulce merchant turned her astonished eyes upon him and stepped away, while at the uproar the innkeeper hurried in from the front, demanding in a loud voice what all the trouble was about.

"It is about a book," said Don Quixote, "which

this unhappy woman, who is no doubt your wife, was destroying under my horrified eyes. Already she has done away with the title page and most of the early leaves; but as I am a scholar, fortunately, I am able to say what book it was. It is, after all, a matter of no great moment, since it is but an account of the life of the low vagabond called Lazarillo of Tormes, who has had the effrontery to imitate the very volume I have for years intended to write. And yet, since it is a book, I cannot stand idly by and allow it to be torn apart. With your permission, I shall ransom the remainder."

Saying which, with a gesture, he flung toward the innkeeper a piece of money which the latter caught and bit between his teeth.

"It is for the book?" asked the owner of the volume.

"And for the bread and wine. Is it not enough?"

"More than enough, your honour. I am your honour's grateful servant."

"Say no more, then; and if there are other volumes about the place, save them for my return. Another bottle, now, to wish us godspeed, for we must be on our way."

They had not ridden far, however, when the ransomed volume, joggling awkwardly beneath the ill-fitting breastplate of the knight, slipped from its place and fell to the earth with a fluttering of leaves. As it fell, a leaf that seemed to have come loose detached itself from the bulk and floated lightly to the side of the road.

"A bad omen," said Sancho Panza, when he had dismounted and handed up the volume. "We are fortunate that it was not a gospel. But, hullo," he cried, plucking the loose leaf from the ground. "What curious plan is this? Beshrew me, Sir Knight, but it looks to me vastly like the outline of my island!" He stared with great earnestness at the square of parchment that he now held in his hand.

"What do you say?" asked his master. "An outline of an island? Hand it to me quickly that I may see whether you have been mistaken."

He looked frowningly upon the drawing that was handed up to him, and tried to read what was written upon its sides.

"It is in a foreign language," he explained, at length. "That is why I do not at once make it out. It is neither Greek nor Latin, nor, I am certain, is it English. What then?"

"French, belike," suggested Sancho Panza. "But certainly it is an island."

"Mount quickly, Sancho," said Don Quixote,

"for this is important. This is a bit of parchment, and has no association with the volume from which it fell. Ride back to the inn and see this innkeeper whom we have just left. Tell him nothing of this map, but ask him how he came by the volume that we purchased. I shall await you here, beneath this tree. By Our Lady, I feel the very breath of enchantments stirring about me! Doubtless, it is the very island that we seek."

Almost before he had finished speaking, the squire was clattering upon his way, and in a short time he was back with the tidings. Beads of perspiration stood out upon his forehead.

"It is the island I am to govern," he cried. "I am sure of it. The book is old, very old. It has been in the possession of this rascally innkeeper for nearly eight years. He had it from a drunken sailor who could not pay his shot. The man was a Portuguese from the place called Funchal in the island called Madeira. He would not say how he had come by the book, but, from our innkeeper's eye, I am certain the fellow stole it and our rascal knows it."

"Hm-m!" muttered the lean knight, and he lay back again against his tree. "There is, at any rate, little likelihood of a dispute about the ownership." He laid his long finger alongside his nose and cast his eyes upward. "Tell me, Friend Sancho, is it your idea that this outline is of the island that is called Madeira?"

"What else? How could it be otherwise? Since it is the island I am to govern, I hope it is large and well stocked with fruits and flowers."

"And no doubt that its women are all young and handsome. I fear me, Sancho, that what you would have is an island wherein one never feels the sting of age or poverty. Such an island as you would like to govern would be a combination, me-thinks, of a Moorish hareem and a banquet hall. You are a sad dog, but I think you are wrong about this plan. If this sailor, drunk or sober, came here from the island of Madeira, would he not know all about that island? What use, then, of a map? And since, instead of remaining in his island of Madeira, he comes to Spain, what are we to sup-pose? It is obvious to me that the island outlined upon this map is close at hand, and that our drunken mariner was seeking it himself."

"So much the better," replied Sancho happily, in response to this flow of wisdom. "Yet why should the dolt part with his map, good sir, in such a case?"

"Idiot!" said Don Quixote. "He did not part

with it willingly. What happened is as plain as the nose upon your face. Now that I come to think of it, I am far from certain that our innkeeper's tale is true. More likely he stole both the book and the map while the drunkard slept."

The little squire sighed profoundly. "What wickedness is in the world!" he cried.

"It is our duty to correct it," returned his master. "For that, we have ventured forth upon this quest. Say nothing, meanwhile, Sancho, of this parchment. I must discover what these writings mean. Silence is golden. Manifold are the dangers of miscellaneous converse. Keep your lips closed tightly. It may be that the hour of your kingdom is at hand."

"What I fear chiefly is that the great admiral, Colon, while seeking the Indies, may stumble upon my island first and take possession of it," said Sancho, with a gloomy shake of his head.

"Nay," answered the knight, "by this, Colon is in the Indies or at the bottom of the sea. He is a wise man and a courageous mariner, but he does ill to seek his islands so far afield. This island that I have promised you is very near."

Greatly rejoicing, they remounted and rode forward under the morning sun, and by midday they had left behind them the fields of Montiel, with their accursed windmills, and were posting happily toward their great adventure.

Not far before them lay the walled town of Seminario, over which ruled a certain duke, both warrior and courtier, and withal a gentleman of very pretty wit. It happened that upon this very day, this nobleman had gone out beyond his walls to hang a thief, in a famous spot set aside for that purpose, and was now returning. So that when the knight of La Mancha and his squire rode over a small hill and beheld not far ahead a vast concourse of people, they quickly reined in their steeds and held a council.

"Surely," cried Don Quixote, clasping his buckler to him, "these are the very hosts of Cæsar returning into Italy. What think you, Sancho? If my eyes do not deceive me, there are captives in their midst whose forlorn estate makes call upon our sympathies."

"Nay," said the squire peaceably, "I see nothing, good sir, but a throng of holiday makers returning to their homes after an outing. What you take to be captives are but swains and sweethearts, locked arm in arm and hip to hip as they advance."

But a strange gleam had appeared in the knight's

eyes, and he answered with a gesture: "Your eyes, Sancho, are like to follow your wits, which are gone glimmering these many years. I tell you these are the myrmidons of Cæsar. Waste no more time in argument, but ride forward at once and acquaint their valiant commander of my coming. Let him select his stoutest knights, and I shall meet them all, one by one or in a body, since I care not a fly for any of them."

Sancho, seeing that his master's mind was made up, rode forward as directed, revolving in his own mind what he should say to the merrymakers when he should have overtaken them. As he came closer, he noted the tall form of a gentleman whom he took to be their leader; and this individual, who was the Duke himself, at the same instant saw the grotesque body of the squire jogging toward him upon a mule. Halting his immediate company, the nobleman awaited the arrival of the mule and its rider with considerable wonderment.

"If I had not some hours ago risen from my bed," said the Duke, "I should believe this stranger some curious figure in a nightmare. He looks for all the world like my fat sow, Niña, that won a prize last year, at Salamanca."

In a few minutes, the squire had ridden into the circle and dismounted. With a low bow, he addressed himself to the nobleman. "Worshipful master," he said, "for my numerous sins, which Heaven forgive me, I serve the maddest gentleman that ever was allowed to roam the earth unaccompanied by a nurse. He calls himself Don Quixote de la Mancha, and he awaits me yonder on the crest of that little hill. It is his insane notion that you and your friends are Cæsar and his armies, no less, and that you have captives whom it is his knightly duty to release. To avoid his rage, I have ridden forward at his request to offer you a challenge."

At this astonishing address, the Duke and his followers burst into a roar of laughter.

"By the Rood, gentleman," cried the Duke, "it will be as good as a play. But you, sir, since you seem to have some sense, why do you attach yourself to so absurd an anachronism as this old scarecrow?"

"Sir," said Sancho, with proper humility, "we are old friends in the same village, and he has at times loaned me small sums of money, which I have been unable to repay; and so I serve him as squire. Besides, he has promised me that in his adventures he will conquer an island for me, over which I shall be made governor and king."

At this the Duke put his hand quickly to his mouth and gravely stroked his long mustachios.

"I see," he said. "I understand! In that case, of course, I cannot blame you. Were it possible, I should assist you, since I can imagine no one more admirably fitted in all respects for either of the eminent positions you have mentioned. Has it occurred to you, perhaps, that your island is somewhere in this neighbourhood?"

"Sir," said Sancho, "these be handsome words," and he again bowed low, and, forgetting all caution, replied: "Indeed, yes; it is exactly as you say. By the strangest chance, we have come into possession of a map of the very island." And he hastened to give the nobleman an account of the parchment and of the manner in which they had come by it.

"A fascinating story," said the Duke. "Present my compliments to your master, if you will, and ask him to do us the honour to join our company. Say to him that we deeply regret the error that the heavy sunlight put upon his eyes; but that, while we are not the myrmidons of Cæsar, we are such gentlemen as he need take no shame to sup with."

As the squire rode off, the nobleman turned in his saddle and smiled upon a knight who sat beside his elbow.

"What do you think of these citizens, Don Juan?" he asked. "Are they as mad as would appear, or spies of his majesty, who still persists in doubting our affection?"

"Mad!" answered the knight addressed. "Mad as my great-aunt Eleanore, who died of it. And yet, their tale is interesting. Do you suppose they have blundered on to something valuable? I should like to see this map, at least."

"We shall both see it presently," said the Duke, "for our knight errant would appear to have accepted our invitation."

In this, however, the Duke was in error, for while Don Quixote was indeed riding toward them, it was with vengeful purpose. He had been greatly wroth with his squire for his betrayal of the map, and was unconvinced that the Duke and his followers were not the armies of Cæsar.

Thus it happened that, as the nobleman gazed across the plain, he saw the incensed adventurer set spurs to his horse and ride toward them at a gallop, followed by the squire upon his mule, shouting and waving his arms. Having already used the only plausible explanation of the occasion, upon the coming of Sancho, the Duke was obliged to assume that, however it might seem, he was actually awake.

As the apparition came nearer, the nobleman saw with amazement that the madman had covered himself with his buckler and rode with his lance against its rest; and the words of the squire came clearly to him on the breeze, bidding them all to flee for their lives. There is no telling what might have happened had not a large stone flung up at that moment by the forehoofs of the thundering Rozinante, struck its rider full upon the mouth, so that the lean knight pitched sidewise out of his saddle and fell senseless upon the earth.

At this catastrophe, the entire company burst out laughing, but in a moment the Duke and some others rode forward to assist Sancho Panza to restore his master to consciousness.

It was quickly discovered that the stone which had caused the mishap had also dashed out two of the Don's teeth, and that he was otherwise in sorry plight as a result of his fall. However, there was still life left within his armour, and after a time he managed to reach his feet without further accident, and to hear the Duke's regrets, which he received with good grace.

"It is perhaps as well that my horse stumbled as he did," said Don Quixote, "inasmuch as the accident enabled me, albeit painfully, to discover my error before I had done any of your party an injury."

"That is possibly true," answered the Duke

politely, "but I regret that the unpremeditated correction of your error should have resulted in the loss of two excellent teeth."

"Do not give it a thought," protested the knight of La Mancha, with a bow. "It is little to lose a few teeth in the service of my Lady Dulcinea, whose favour I wear, and in the service of Him who has given me all my teeth. Our Lord, who reared this fabric, has but opened a window in order to discern more readily what passes within."

"You are a philosopher," said the Duke, with admiration.

"My squire, Sancho Panza, who has little wit and chatters a great deal," said Don Quixote, "tells me that he has already acquainted you with our situation and has given you tidings of our quest. As for the small matter of the map, I should not have thought it worthy to call to your attention."

"No doubt it is a trifling matter," agreed the Duke, "and yet so curious a landfall deserves investigation. Your squire informs me that, your languages being rusty, you have been unable wholly to translate the sense of the document. May I offer my small French and little English in your service?"

"Your Lordship is too kind! Here is the parchment, none the worse for its fall. Sancho, I see the hand of Providence in this."

"The very finger of God," said Sancho Panza, and he ambled quickly to the side of the Duke's stallion that he might lose no word that fell from the lips of the savant.

The Duke's eyes, as he turned the parchment in his fingers, had narrowed, and now looked with curious regard into those of his friend whom he had previously addressed.

"A quaint and pretty thing," he said idly, after a moment, "and as you surmise, the language is French. By the most extraordinary good fortune, you have hit upon the very spot you seek. The island is no more than a league beyond us, across the brow of yonder hill. I am well acquainted with it, but was unaware that it was without a governor."

"It is *here?*" shrieked Sancho Panza, in an ecstasy. "Holy Virgin, are you telling me that my island is here awaiting me?"

"No more than an hour's ride from where we stand. 'Twill be a peaceable conquest, I fancy, since its people are in no wise warlike. I and my friends would have pleasure in acting as your escort."

As he spoke, the nobleman passed the parchment

to his friend, who, after a moment, whistled softly in amazement, and turned aside to hide the fierce light in his eyes.

Having said all that appeared to be necessary, and without giving the new governor or his master opportunity for either gratitude or protest, the Duke called his followers about him in such fashion that on all sides they fell in about the pair of citizens from La Mancha. Thus patterned, the party rode rapidly forward toward the walled town of Seminario, into which the holiday makers already had preceded them. As they rode, the Duke glanced downward from time to time at the parchment map that he carried in his hand, and, after a while, he placed it inside his doublet for safer keeping.

A great outpouring of inhabitants cheered as they rode in through the gates, and the bosoms of Sancho Panza and Don Quixote swelled proudly at the tumult. On all sides, the islanders surged and shouted. From the balconies, the girls and women tossed roses and poppies down. The entire municipality seemed to be in a state of carnival. Flags and bunting draped the fronts of the houses, and across the principal thoroughfare was stretched a broad placard, advertising the virtues of a popular candidate for office.

"They are cheering you as their new governor," whispered the Duke to the squire. "See how they have hung your portrait over the street! Take off your hat and bow to them. That is right. Note how they laugh. They are pleased by your appearance. Gaze gratefully upon that glorious creature who hangs from yonder balcony. She is quite mad about you. Ah, there are some charming girls in your kingdom, lucky fellow! I am beginning to envy you."

"They are but bags of trouble," observed the knight of La Mancha. "You will do well, Sancho, to leave them alone. For my part, I have been done with them these many years, and am all the wiser for it."

"Sir Knight," said the Duke, "it has been a happiness to know you. Doubtless, you are quite right. But I regret that here I must turn aside. Stubborn matters await me, and I must deny myself the further pleasure of your company. My friend, Don Juan Perez de Ortubia, will continue with you to the palace gates. And so farewell!"

"My map!" cried Don Quixote, with sudden dismay. "What of my map, Lord Duke?"

"You will not need it now; but still, it is yours. Let me have it for only a day or two. There is a word that still escapes me. I promise you, I shall return it in person."

With a flourish of his gloved hand, he rode off, followed by half of the glittering company, while Don Quixote and his squire continued across the town to its farther gate, having passed through which, they were kicked heartily from the rear and told to go about their business.

CHAPTER FOUR

IN WHICH GREAT SEARCH IS MADE FOR A FOUNTAIN

Whither in your bowl so free?
To rake the moon from out the sea.
—T. L. PEACOCK.

Juan Ponce, of the ancient house of León, swung moodily in his hammock beneath the trees. He had divested himself of his weight of armour, and his thick legs hung down on either side of the swing as if he still sat upon his charger's back. His ageing stomach flowed forward and sat upon his lap. In the sunny garden, rare birds sang and fluttered their wings, and beyond the crenellated parapet of the wall, the heaving waters of the bay, tinted with indigo, washed soothingly against the masonry. Had he looked landward from his island home, he would have gazed upon a palm-fringed coast, sweeping away in narrowing perspective to the higher hills.

But the governor of Porto Rico was sullen and depressed. Indeed, he was no longer governor of

Porto Rico. That morning, his titles had been taken from him and now dignified the very scoundrel he had sent home to Spain in disgrace. Such are the ways of princes and of queens. The wonder was, he reflected morosely, that they had not stripped him of his castle and his lands.

An idea occurred to him. At least he was his own master now. He might come and go exactly as he pleased. He clapped his hands and bawled lustily from his hammock, and a soldier came running.

"Bring me the Carib woman, Pablo," said the ex-Governor of Porto Rico. "The *vieja* who was here a week ago. I ordered her to be detained."

"Certainly, Excellency," bowed the soldier. "The old one with the withered breast. The Doña Inez has put her to work in the kitchen." He hastened away.

Juan Ponce pulled reflectively at his beard, twisting his mouth into doubtful lines. He looked with dissatisfaction upon his distended paunch, and touched with his fingers the thinning hair upon his head.

"At any rate," he murmured, "it is worth a chance. Almost anything that happened to me would be in the nature of an improvement. Inez is right: I am much too fat. This sedentary life is not good for me. A brisk adventure is what I need, with plenty of fighting. I wonder if this miraculous water is potent against the ravage of a sword-thrust. No matter, if it makes one young. If this woman is not lying, now . . ."

He looked up and saw her coming toward him across the garden, accompanied by the energetic Pablo. She was incredibly ugly, and he viewed her seamed and toothless face with disfavour. The Carib woman was bowing repeatedly as she approached, uncertain what the summons portended. In a moment, she stood before him, clad in one of his wife's old wrappers, which he recognized with a sense of shock.

"You may go, Pablo," said Juan Ponce, with a wave of dismissal. To the Carib woman, in her own tongue, he said: "Tell me again about that island!"

A light of understanding appeared in the crone's eyes. She smiled hideously. Turning, she pointed away to the northern horizon.

There was an island. It was called by the name of Bimini. At its heart, a spring gushed forth in an unfailing stream, to bathe in which was to receive the gift of youth. Years before, a war canoe had gone upon the voyage and never had returned. The warriors who sailed it were Caribs and kinsmen of her own. They had heard of an isle of fruit and flowers, and of a fountain that flowed from out of its bosom whose waters were as the breath of life. But they had never come back. Therefore, they had found the fountain of rejuvenescence, for they were brave and skilful sailors that neither man nor tempest could detain against their will.

"Ah-h-h!" breathed the veteran. In a moment he said: "It sounds a trifle like a priest's tale of the Garden of Eden. Might it not be that these warriors who were your kinsmen were slain before they reached the island?"

But the old woman shook her head. They were mighty warriors, she insisted. They might slay, but they would not be slain. Among them were old men and old women, who had been taken on the voyage that the virtue of the waters might be tested. More than a year after they had vanished, there had been word of them. A trading canoe, visiting at Boriquen, had brought the tidings. The traders had passed an island, far to the north, upon which they had seen and talked with old men who had been restored to riotous youth, and beldames who had regained the virginal bloom of girlhood. There was no doubt at all that they were her missing kinsmen.

"Why, then, do they not return?" demanded the Conquistadore.

It was very simple, the woman said. They were afraid to come home because of the scandal their youthful appearance would work among their friends.

Juan Ponce wheezed and got upon his feet. For some moments, he tramped backward and forward across the garden, tugging at his mouth. At length he stopped before the story-teller and fixed her with his glance.

"And you can lead me there?" he asked.

"It is as clear within my brain," she answered, "as my own cabin and the path that leads up to the door. I have often heard our warriors speak of it, and how to find it."

"You shall go with us, then, to point the way!"

The Carib woman nodded her head and smiled. "Now that I am old," she said, "what does it matter where I dwell? Whether on land or on the water, I am at the master's service. I care not about the fountain for myself, for my life already has been hard and long, and I would not wish to live it over again. But I will show you the way."

"So be it," decreed Juan Ponce; and he began to wonder what his wife would say. "Tell nothing to anyone about what I have spoken."

He dismissed her to her tasks, and reseating

himself in the hammock, gave himself over to thought. There were three caravels in the port, and they were at his disposal. No doubt there would be trouble with the new governor, but that was unimportant. The new governor might go to China, or fry himself in oil. Enlistment terms had most of them expired, and the men were free to venture as they wished. "'*Por donde va la mar, vayan las arenas,*'" quoth Juan Ponce. "Where the sea goes, there the sands go. They cannot stop me!"

What his wife had to say was a great deal.

"You sailed with Colon on this ridiculous quest," she pointed out, "and what came of it? Is Colon a young man wooing the Queen's Majesty under her husband's nose? I think not. He is in his grave these six years, where I imagine he wishes he had let well enough alone. I thought you had got over your silly notion about a fountain of youth."

"We failed, it is true," agreed Juan Ponce, "but had not his enemies at court ruined the good Colon, who can say what might have happened? He died, not of old age, but of a broken heart."

"He is no less dead for that," said his wife. "Upon my word," she cried angrily, "you are getting to be a greater fool every day. On the very day you lose your position as governor of

Porto Rico, you must decide upon some such absurd adventure as this to occupy your time. If it is your waistline that you are bewailing, there are plenty of waters near at hand to reduce it. The truth is, you eat too much, and lie around in a hammock when you should be taking a brisk ride. My word upon it, Juan Ponce, if you leave me and the children again, I shall be off with the first rich cacique who asks me."

But Juan Ponce, who was very fond of his wife, and knew her quite as well as she knew herself, was not alarmed about her conduct in his absences. He put his arm around her and gently patted her shoulder.

"There, there, my dear," he said, "if you forbid me, of course I shall not go. It is a selfish quest, I must admit. Were I seeking these waters for *your* sake, then indeed it would be an idle venture, for *your* youth has never left you. And yet, were I to succeed where Colon failed—and that at once, after they have tried to disgrace me—I think there is no preferment in the Queen's power that might not be ours."

For a moment, she laid her head against his doublet and twined her fingers in his beard.

"You are an old idiot, Juan Ponce," she answered softly, "and you satisfy me sufficiently as you are; but, if you must go, then I suppose you must. I shall burn candles for your return."

Thus it came about that there was a great bustle at the castle of San Juan, and a great slaughtering of hogs and cattle. From the country round about came troops of Indians with provisions for the voyage. Cannon were mounted on the decks of the caravels, ammunition was stored in their holds, and from all points clustered the adventurers of the islands to offer their swords to the cavalier who quested after youth. "For," said these latter, "while it is possible that Juan Ponce is an elderly jackass, it is certain that there will be adventures in plenty, and quite possibly much gold."

Juan Ponce kissed his wife and family affectionately before leaving them behind.

"Look well upon me, Inez," he said merrily, "for when I return it will be as a young and handsome *caballero*. Do not be jealous, however, for I shall bring with me some of the waters of the spring, and when you have partaken also, we shall renew our honeymoon."

"I shall be satisfied," answered his wife, "if you return with a whole skin. It is your eating and drinking that is at fault, rather than your age. However, God and Our Lady keep you."

"I shall come back a beardless stripling,"

boasted the veteran. "We shall return to Spain with water for Their Majesties and all the court."

"So Colon thought," responded the Doña Inez, "although his intentions were less munificent than your own. Already I hear the chains rattling on your ankles."

"Colon failed," retorted her husband. "I have told you how it happened, many times. By his failure, the fountain was supposed to have been proved a fable. It was thought he had lied to gain his selfish ends. Now it is different. Do not doubt the story of this excellent woman who accompanies me; it is as true as that the sun goes round the earth. Farewell, my love! You will know me upon my return by the memory of our wooing."

With a ludicrous bow, he lumbered on board his caravel and gave the order to cast off. When the three vessels had passed out of the roadstead, the Doña Inez touched her eyes with her handkerchief and rode homeward.

"Your father," she observed to her children, as they returned to the castle of San Juan, "is a most amiable and excellent gentleman, but uncommonly impractical and visionary. He has been a good provider, I am bound to admit, but he has been chasing will-o'-the wisps ever since we were married. This voyage will cost us a pretty penny and

will put nothing in our pockets. I am thankful that
we have a roof over our heads."

There were no doubts, however, in the mind of
Juan Ponce, as he paced the deck of his flagship;
and even when two months had passed over his
head, leaving it no younger, and still the island of
Bimini had not risen from the sea, he did not de-
spair. Standing massively beside his pilot, the
dependable Anton de Alminos, he took counsel
with that mariner and uttered words of caution.

"Anton," he said, "we were both with Colon
and are familiar with his researches. He was a
wise man and an excellent seaman. We must be
careful not to travel foolishly in his tracks. It is
the islands Colon *missed* that we have to search for,
and so come at length to Bimini. Nevertheless, I
grant you that they are all most damnably similar."

"Assuredly, Excellency," answered the pilot.
"I have had several conversations with the *vieja*,
and we are still some distance from that island.
It lies farther to the northward and westward.
Yet it might be well to land at all such places as
are unknown to us, since, after all, this old woman
has never been there herself. Twice she has been
deceived by the absurd clouds that form so curiously on the horizon as to seem like islands. I

hope the old devil knows what she is talking about."

"*Por Dios!*" exploded the commander, looking savagely across the waste of shining water, "if she has deceived us, she shall be turned adrift upon one of her own cloud banks, with the sky for company." He heaved a sigh. "It is a pity, Anton, that so many of these islets we have visited should be so well supplied with water. If it were but a single spring we had to seek, and there were no other, how happily it would simplify matters! As it is, every island must have its fountain, and some of them two or three. Any one of them may be the one we quest. I have drunk so deeply at them all that I loathe the very sight of water. Holy Mother! I warrant a caravel might float upon the water that I have drunk!"

The pilot looked critically at his employer's jowls.

"It has done you no harm, Excellency, if I may say so. I believe, verily, that you are somewhat more youthful than when we sailed."

"You are very knd, Anton; but there is, alas, still room for improvement. I no longer deceive myself. Yet once I wore the Queen's favour and jousted with the best of them. I remember a day in Burgos—and a woman with a black shawl—

but I was newly married, then, and not to be tempted. The retrospects of life, Anton, teem with lost opportunities. Why must one think of them as age advances? Youth is a disease, and we should be very glad to be quit of it."

But when another island had been sighted, somewhat of the commander's spirits revived, and he was the first to spring ashore and drink deeply of the central stream. When six long months had drifted by, however, and still there had been no sign of the spot called Bimini, Juan Ponce's enthusiasm waned. Calling the Carib woman to his side, he spoke sharply to her.

"Does this island of yours have legs that it may walk?" he asked. "Does it have fins that it may swim, or wings that it may fly? Is it forever sailing away from us?"

Still she pointed to the northward, with trembling finger; and suddenly, while still her finger was outstretched, there sounded a sharp cry from the lookout. Another island was rising above the ocean rim. At the word, the commander gave over his inquiry and the entire company rushed forward to the bows.

"Is it land, Anton, or another cloud wreath?" growled Juan Ponce. "If it moves or floats upward, doubtless it is the island of Bimini."

The pilot stared across the intervening miles of water, and the old woman, shading her eyes with her hand, looked also at the low shape that was slowly rising out of the sea.

"It is land, Excellency," answered the pilot, at last. "It is a new island. I have never been here before."

All eyes were now turned upon the face of the *vieja*, who still stared from beneath the shadow of her hand. There was a long silence. Then the ancient lips began to writhe, and suddenly with a smile and a cry she turned upon her master.

"I think," said the Carib woman, "it is the island of Bimini."

With a shout, Juan Ponce hurled his cap into the ocean and clasped the astonished native in his arms.

"We are victorious!" he cried. "God in His mercy has answered our prayers. A cask of youth to every man on board! Meanwhile, a small libation for our greater cheer. Be ready, Anton, to signal the other vessels; it may be that they have not yet observed this miracle."

All morning the vessels sailed onward, and shortly after midday dropped anchor at the southern extremity of a fertile wooded island, from the centre of which rose a lofty hill. Whereupon all hands were turned out and repeated the *Gloria in excelsis Deo*, after which a generous ration of rum was served to the crew and strict orders were issued that no man was to leave the caravel without the commander's orders.

A short time later, a small boat put out from each of the three vessels and the officers met upon the beach.

"Gentlemen," said the commander, "the instructions are as always: whoever shall discover a stream or spring of fresh water shall immediately send word of his discovery to me. No one is to touch his lips to water, on penalty of death, until I have first tasted it. Aliminos and the *vieja* will accompany me with half a dozen men. Juan Perez de Ortubia will lead his party along the shore and join us on the farther side. You, Don Luis, must remain here upon the beach, that we may not lose contact with the ships. . . . It is a strange thing, Anton," he added, "that we have seen no natives. Usually they are to be found awaiting our approach. Do they no longer have periwinkles for sale? It would be a surprising paradox if all our immortals had perished."

The tall hill rose upward at no great distance, and on its paths could be seen innumerable goats, frisking and feeding in the warm sunshine. Trees of splendid height, luxuriant and blossoming, swayed their tops in the breeze; the air was heavy with their fragrance. Bright-hued birds flashed through the branches and called their melodies. But the riotous youths and the rejuvenated beldames lolled in no shameful ease upon the swards; they were nowhere within view. The island seemed barren of all human life, save only the adventurers' selves.

"Unless," muttered Juan Ponce, with a feeling of disquiet, "they have in some fashion been changed into goats!" Turning upon the Carib woman, he asked: "Where are your friends, old woman?"

The *vieja* was undisturbed. "No doubt they have gone into hiding," she answered calmly. "Our approach has frightened them away. In time, we shall find them. Perhaps they are even now gathered at the never-failing spring."

It was an idea that had escaped the commander, and he accepted it. The order to advance was given, and with a cheer the searching parties moved forward upon their missions. But the tangled thicket that lay before Juan Ponce and his party seemed to forbid all access to the interior. With swords and knives they hacked into the stout bushes and vines, and cutting a path before them,

progressed slowly toward the base of the mountain.
Birds and small animals fled before them, or gazed
fearfully with bright eyes from secret recesses of
the jungle. The sun, for the most part hidden by
the trees, was still felt at every step, and a myriad
of tiny insects danced and hummed in the gloom.

In time, they came upon a rough trail that led in
zigzag fashion around and upward, as if into the
heart of the mountain. Overhead the trees still
met and intertwined, and in their path the coiling
vines and creepers were twisted and laced like
emerald serpents. They toiled forward in green
obscurity, at times pierced and dappled by the
heavy sunlight, at times dim and mysterious as
the back curtain of a dream.

But the huge figure of Juan Ponce, crashing
through the brush, contained small thought of the
strangenesses of the way. Hot and panting, dripping with perspiration, what he listened for was
the soothing fall of water upon rock, or the running
of a crystal stream among stones and pebbles.

When more than an hour had passed, they came
upon a cleared space, ringed by trees, and then a
wider path that led quickly into another patch
of thicket. It savoured of habitation. Heartened by
the sight, they pushed rapidly forward, to hear
presently with wonder and apprehension the roar

of water beating with great fists against the rocks. It was a tremendous sound that seemed almost to be beneath their feet.

"Can it be the fountain?" cried Juan Ponce, in amazement. "By its sound and volume, it is very like the sea!"

They blundered upon another path, the work of human hands, and following it closely came quickly out upon the other side of the island. Before them lay the open sea, beating at this point with great noise upon the rocks below. A thin fog of spray rose upward and spread abroad, and from the height at which they stood the wide panorama of rolling, tossing water was visible to an immense distance.

Their path ended abruptly at the cliff's edge, but another was seen at a small distance, tortuously climbing the side of the mountain: a steep and rugged trail that must have been the playground of the goats. Down this fantastic pathway, as they gazed, came climbing the brown figure of a native, with a loincloth, at sight of which they cried out in astonishment, for by its long white hair and hanging breasts it was the figure of an old woman. The creature paused at sight of the invaders, and for a moment viewed them at a distance; then she came rapidly on, climbing with extraordinary agility for one of her evident age. As she came closer, they saw that she was even more ancient than their own *vieja*, and if possible more ugly.

This final disappointment, after the months of questing, was too much for Juan Ponce. He sat himself down upon a stone and sighed wearily.

"Gentlemen," he observed, with pathetic humour, "if this young female who approaches has achieved her maidenhood at the perpetual spring, you may have her, and the water, too, for what purpose you will. My blessings be upon you!" And with great accuracy, he spat far outward and into the sea.

The *vieja* was shaking her head doubtfully. Suddenly she tottered forward and advanced upon the other woman. The crones approached each other warily. At a distance of several hundred feet they stopped, and the Carib woman began to scream her inquiries and the other to reply. In time, they met without malice, and the conversation was continued. They waved their arms with great earnestness and urgency, the one pointing upward to the mountain crest, the other across the water to the west. Then the Carib woman limped painfully back to her master, and, prostrating herself before him, made her report.

There was an island. It was called Bimini. It lay far to the northward and westward. At its heart, a running spring gushed forth from the rock, the waters of which——

With a magnificent oath, Juan Ponce got upon his feet. "The devil fly away with you!" he said. "I have had enough of this nonsense. I have drunk water and more water until it is a wonder that I am not a fish. I have followed one old woman until it is a wonder I am not an old woman, myself. I shall not follow another. I am through. As a matter of fact, I am going home. Inez was right. I am an elderly idiot. If any of you gentlemen care to continue this insane search for what does not exist, you have my permission and my blessing. I am going back to Boriquen and drink wine for the rest of my life."

"Still," demurred Anton de Aliminos, "two heads are notoriously better than one. This other creature, who is even older than our own *vieja*, is very positive. It is, at least, a striking coincidence that our own old woman, in erring, should have led us to an island whereon we have found another, even more aged, who also knows the story. There may be something in it, Excellency. With two of them to guide us, there is no telling what we may not find."

"With two of them to guide us," responded Juan Ponce, "may God help us. His finger has been notably absent in this adventure, from the beginning. However, Anton, I will toss a *real* with you to determine whether we are to go forward for a final effort, or turn homeward upon the first breeze. Heads, we go forward to this other island, which shall be the last; tails, we make all speed for Boriquen and a comfortable hammock."

"Done!" said the pilot. "Upon one condition, however: that *you* shall produce the *real*."

The coin was flung in a circle of interested officers, and falling upon its edge, rolled quickly over the cliff and into the sea. A second was more fortunate for Anton: it fell head up, and, dusting his knees, the Conquistadore arose.

"God's hand, at last, perhaps," said he. "It is now a case of three heads being better than one. I shall no longer oppose my own to the programme. We sail at daybreak."

So it came about that, voyaging steadily northward and westward, in obedience to the guidance of the second *vieja*, who was now in favour, they came actually at last upon an island that was called by the name of Bimini. This time there could be no possible doubt about it. Not only did both of the commander's old women agree that the spot had been found, but the natives of the place themselves insisted that it could not be otherwise. Whereupon, Juan Ponce fell upon his knees, with his men around him, and took possession of the island and all its people, in the names of the King and Queen of Spain, whom Heaven preserve.

It was a green and level strand that they had come upon, bright with gay trees and singing birds; and in the centre there shimmered beneath the sun a broad and placid lagoon, kneeling beside which Juan Ponce clutched aside his beard and endeavoured to bend his body to the water. His girth, by this time, was so great that even this simple feat had become impossible, and with vast groaning he was obliged to lower himself flat upon the sand, and so lying, push his face forward and downward into the stream.

"It is surprisingly like all other water that I have tasted," he admitted, when he had been assisted to his feet. "If anything, I should say a trifle flatter," he added critically. "Nevertheless, if it be the veritable fountain of youth, it should not be long before I begin to show its effect. Fill up the hogsheads, Don Luis, and see to it that one is safely bestowed in my cabin. In time, gentlemen, you shall all have your share, but for the nonce our duty is to Their Majesties. By the saints, I believe that already I feel the glow of youth stealing through me! Tell me, Anton, does it strike you that my appearance is, if anything, more youthful?"

"Infinitely so, Excellency. You have within an instant dropped a dozen years."

"Perhaps it is merely the triumph of discovery," continued the commander cautiously, "and yet I swear I feel a very boy again."

"What bothers me, Excellency," ventured one of the officers, "is the strangely familiar appearance of these natives. There are among them men and women of all ages, much as at home and elsewhere."

"Tush!" cried Juan Ponce, with a snap of his fingers. "They are like our *vieja*, many of them. They do not care to relive their lives. Since they are destined to be our slaves, I am not sure that I greatly blame them. Perhaps Their Majesties will make the drinking of this elixir compulsory. Thus one slave might be made to go a long way. It is a plan that I must be careful to suggest. This is a great day for the world, gentlemen, and to the end of time the name of Ponce de León will be associated with it. I am perhaps the greatest benefactor the human race will ever see."

"And yet," said Anton de Aliminos, "I have heard it said that youth is a disease."

"Anton," said his commander, "beware how you taunt me, or you shall have none of it. It is age that is the disease, and I have found its remedy."

Meanwhile, there adventured in another part of the island, Juan Perez de Ortubia, who had been left behind to keep open the line of communication. With a single trusted follower he had slipped away upon one pretext or another, and now stood with gleaming eyes beside a cleft rock from which gushed a single stream of crystal fluid. It was the fountain of perpetual youth. Juan Perez had known where to find it. On his person he still carried the map of François Villon, stolen by his master from the knight of La Mancha, some years before. Twice, under orders from his duke, he had sailed with the ill-starred Colon upon quests that came always to nothing, and at length he had attached himself to the household of Juan Ponce. His duke was dead, at last. Juan Perez de Ortubia, alone of all men living, possessed the secret of the fountain. Lucky Juan Perez!

He glanced quickly about him, while his single retainer stood guard some distance from the rock. The little stream welled forth with a freshness and a clarity that seemed fraught with a sense of its significance. What thoughts filled the breast of him who stood there, trembling! Stooping, he cupped his hands to the water and drank eagerly from his palms. A fierce glow seemed to fill his veins; it tingled through him like the warmth of old wines. With difficulty, he restrained his shout of triumph. Then, thrusting a hand deeply into the skirt of his cloak, he brought forth a glittering golden vial. It was studded about its throat with gleaming jewels and sealed at its extremity with a jewelled stopper. In length, it was no more than six inches from end to end; in girth, no thicker than his thumb. Yet it would hold enough of the precious, the miraculous liquid to restore a regiment to youth. A single drop was sufficient to strike away the fetters of a decade. So François Villon had written.

Sealing the vial firmly, when he had filled it from the spring, Juan Perez restored it to its hiding place and rejoined his companion. "It is done, Sebastian," he whispered. "Only you and I shall ever know." And he drove his dagger into the heart of Sebastian, who fell dead at his feet.

To his commander, when they came face to face, Juan Perez said:

"From my heart, I offer congratulations, Excellency. It is fortunate, is it not, that so famous a spring should have so large and public a surface?"

"What mean you by that, Don Juan?" asked his commander.

"Only that it is likely to become a popular resort."

Juan Ponce watched him as he departed to his ship. There was a swagger about the fellow that was irritating.

"I distrust that man, Anton," said Juan Ponce. "There was something hidden beneath his words that savoured of mockery. Is he jealous of my success?"

"Who is not, Excellency?" answered the pilot politely. "I think I am a little jealous, myself."

Juan Perez de Ortubia was at this time close upon his thirty-second year, and so youthful in appearance that the change worked upon him went unnoticed, save that the extraordinary ebullience of his spirits was remarked and charged against his vanity. How long he was able to retain the youth with which he had overwhelmed himself is part of what is yet to be told.

CHAPTER FIVE

IN WHICH THERE IS A SCANDAL AT THE COURT

> *The King was in his counting house,*
> *Counting out his money;*
> *The Queen was in the pantry,*
> *Eating bread and honey.*
> —MOTHER GOOSE.

We have seen how one Queen of Spain, looking into a mirror and seeing that which did not please her, was willing to pawn her jewels for a trifle of youth. But there are queens and queens. We shall see now how another Queen of Spain, similarly consulting, found that within her glass which pleased her greatly.

Germaine, princess of France, second venture of King Ferdinand, was not yet thirty and very beautiful, when Juan Perez de Ortubia, that youthful cavalier, returning from his triumph, looked gratefully into her eyes and found her more lovely than any of her maids-in-waiting. Without waste of time, he made his addresses and found her not insensible to his own attractions. Thereafter, the world went very well for both of them, although before it had seemed dreary enough.

It is not to be supposed, however, that this second discovery by Juan Perez, of a fountain of youth within the very palace of the King, was attended by public recognition of so auspicious an event. In point of fact, it was surrounded by a secrecy almost as profound as that which had enveloped his first triumph. The Queen and Juan Perez themselves knew, having been present on the occasion of the discovery; a few maids suspected, and the excellent successor to the lamented Sebastian, who dressed his master for the royal visits, was certain that something of a delightful nature was going forward. It was a triumph that could not be kept secret for long, however, and in time some gossip of the matter reached the ears of the King and deeply annoyed him.

Yet the fault was none other than His Majesty's own. Juan Perez had returned in a delicate moment. A single drop of the precious liquid he carried, bestowed at this time upon the aging Ferdinand, might have changed the history of Europe. But Juan Perez, locking his secret even from the Queen's Majesty, allowed the physicians to work their will upon his monarch, who, under their ministrations, became increasingly despairful. Thus it fell out that the King discovered himself in an embarrassing and paradoxical position. Deeply desiring a son and heir to carry on his infirmities, he was desperately afraid that he might have one.

In this juncture, there appeared before the court at Burgos, asking audience, an elderly gentleman with a gray beard and a bald head, exceedingly stiff in the joints, who carried his abdomen before him like a drum. He came to make report of his deeds beyond the horizon. In the antechambers of the palace, the courtiers rallied about him.

"Kind Justice!" said the younger ones, "it is actually the valiant Juan Ponce himself, he who quested the fountain of youth! Look upon him, gentlemen, and weep. He would appear to have drunk all the waters of the Indies."

A beardless youth, dripping perfume, touched him upon the arm. "How is this, Juan Ponce?" he asked. "I was a boy when you went away from us. Now I am grown, and you, who went away a veteran, return to us a youth with flowing locks. Can it be that you have discovered the secret of youth, and is the recipe for sale?"

"The callow striplings," muttered Juan Ponce contemptuously. "Little beard, little modesty."

Aloud he said: "In less than a thousand years, gentlemen, we shall all be bald."

The older gallants laughed and fluttered their hands in applause, and a lady who had been close to the former queen smiled graciously. "Your heart, Juan Ponce," she said, "is no older than when last you laid it at my feet."

"As I do now, Madame," responded the veteran, with an awkward bow.

But, as they thronged around him to ask about his adventures, an attendant came from the royal presence to command him to appear before the King. In a moment, he was in the reception chamber and kneeling before his sovereign.

"I am glad to see you, Juan Ponce," said Ferdinand. "Rise up and sit here beside me. Your fame has preceded you. On all sides they trumpet your renown. But you return no younger, I fear; nor do you find your king a sparkling youngster. You remind me of a happier day. Tell me of your triumphs. I can give you half an hour." He lay back in his great chair and regarded the soldier with shrewd, suspicious eyes.

"I can tell you in less time than that, Majesty," answered the veteran bluntly. "Her late lamented Majesty, whom God rest, was interested in Colon's fable of a magic fountain. Deeply as I deplore her passing, I am spared the embarrassment of reporting a further failure. The place exists; I have stood beside its waters. They were no more potent than our own. For two years I have awaited their effect upon my person. The result sits enormously before you."

The King smiled. "I guessed as much from your dispatches. You have my sympathy. Her late Majesty was very fond of you, and often spoke of you with kindness. Yet I regret to hear your confirmation of reports of your ill success. I have need of such waters!"

"Instead, I beg to offer Your Majesty some sixty islands of the sea, and the continent of Florida. Instead of water, fruits, slaves, and precious metals."

"They no longer interest me," said the King, "but you have done well, I make no doubt, and shall be rewarded. The waters are quite impotent?"

"As a talisman of youth, quite! For casual ablutions, and for drinking when there is no wine to be had, they are excellent, although no better than are to be found elsewhere. Your Majesty's new lands, however——"

"A pox on them!" said the King. "Had you but

brought me a small vial of youth, good Ponce, even three tiny drops, you should have deserved rewards that would have beggared me. As it is——"

He frowned sharply, and a mad gleam appeared in his deep-set eyes. "Tell me of one who followed in your train. One Perez de Ortubia! What do you know of that young man?"

"He is here in Spain," replied the veteran. "He left the islands some months ago."

"He is here at court," corrected the King. "I know him passing well. He is an attractive and accomplished cavalier. Her Majesty, also, is very fond of him. But what of his conduct in the islands? Was it in all ways exemplary and that of a loyal captain?"

Juan Ponce, embarrassed, tugged at his beard. "Your Majesty's inquisition puzzles me," he answered. "It is true that I do not greatly like the man, although how you have discovered that I cannot guess; but, in all respects, he was an excellent officer. I have no complaint to make."

"Why do you not like him?" asked the King eagerly. "That is what I wish to hear. Between ourselves, I do not like him overwell, myself."

"And that is what I cannot tell you," said the veteran. "I do not know. It is something in his manner, I think. Perhaps in the fall of his cloak.

Perhaps it is only the arrogance of youth, of which I have just had a taste in Your Majesty's ante-chambers; it is ever self-satisfied and inconsiderate of age. It encompasses the wisdom of the ages, and their intolerance. This youth! And yet how eagerly we expose ourselves to its contagion when we have come to forty years! Does not Your Majesty find it so? Alas, we shall never either of us see forty again—or fifty! Believe me, Sire, the Doña Inez was right when she advised me against the venture. It is her notion that youth is not to be recaptured by violence or by charms. And yet, for six months it bubbled within me, what time I sought its source at the fountain of Bimini. It would bubble again, were I to attempt another quest, to-morrow. And why? Because it is not of the flesh, Majesty, but of the spirit. It renews itself at the fountains of our ideals and our passions, which are within us."

"You are become quite a philosopher, Ponce," observed the King drily. "You will not mind if I do not entirely agree with you? My experience runs contrary to your philosophy. In what way may I serve you?"

"My philosophy goes even deeper, Majesty, since it has taught me, at length, the folly of quest-ing the unattainable. And so I ask no more than that I may be permitted to return to my castle in Boriquen. I begin to miss my hammock and my children and the company of my wife."

The King of Spain rose quickly to his feet and paced about the chamber.

"All in good time, Juan Ponce," he answered. "We still have need of you in our service. You shall be governor of the lands that you have discovered, and in time shall remove your hammock and your family whither you will. In respect, however, to your officer, Ortubia: he was with you upon this quest?"

"He commanded a caravel."

"Then his opportunities were no greater and no less than your own. It would not have been possible for him to succeed where yourself had failed?"

For a moment the veteran sat blinking. "Had any but Your Majesty hazarded the suggestion," he replied, at length, "I should have thought him to be jesting."

"It is impossible, then?"

"Quite impossible!"

The King breathed deeply and resumed his seat. "It is of no importance," he explained, "but it is the marvel of the court how he retains his youth. I have watched him in the field and at the games. Tell me, good Ponce, with reference to this water that does not exist: is its magic effective against a sword thrust or an hempen cord?"

"It is curious that the same thought was once in my own mind," exclaimed the soldier. "I cannot say, of course, since the legend is not clear upon the point."

"It is an interesting point, however," smiled the King of Spain. "I commend it to the attention of scholars. My respects to your lady, Ponce, when you shall have returned to Boriquen. Say nothing, meanwhile, to Ortubia—or to anyone else—of our conversation. The Queen of Spain and her ladies await your presence in her apartments. They perish of ennui," he added sardonically, "and would hear the story of the romantic cavalier who sought youth rather than gold."

"By your command, Majesty," answered the veteran, "since God knows I have few social talents. My experience of the sex has been small."

"Without it your philosophy is incomplete," said the King. "Farewell, Ponce, and say to Her Majesty that I shall not join her for the recital."

Bowing for the last time upon the threshold, the stout knight was aware that already he had lost the King's attention. In his dark raiment of the people, Ferdinand stood morosely thumbing his chin before a window that overlooked the courtyard. Save for the splendour of his surroundings, he looked like one of his own peasants of Aragon.

At the entrance to Germaine's apartments, Juan Ponce paused and listened to the apologies of Her Majesty's secretary. The Queen of Spain was, unfortunately, engaged at the moment, and had been obliged to postpone the audience to Ponce de León. Deeply relieved, the veteran retreated, and as he turned away there brushed quickly past him, and past the secretary, a slender and gorgeous youth, who, with a nod and smile of recognition, vanished behind the hangings. It was Juan Perez de Ortubia. From behind the silken barrier sounded the fluttering laugh of a woman.

Vastly perturbed, Juan Ponce fled the scene, and blundering twice in his haste into forbidden chambers, reached the fresh air again.

"By Saint James!" said the veteran, "the King's riddles are less puzzlesome than I had thought. Inez was right. I am no figure for a courtier. I should have stayed at home."

Reaching his caravels, moored in the harbour, he sought his own cabin and sat down with considerable relief.

Meanwhile, in the audience chamber that he had just quitted, another scene was in progress. The curtains had been drawn and the court loungers had been excluded. Across a table, Their Majesties of Spain faced each other warily. They were as alone as if they had been together in their common bedchamber, yet their words were as artfully chosen as if they had been surrounded on every hand by listeners. Unwilling to interrupt the lady at her dalliance, lest he should be made aware of it, the King had summoned his consort to the presence.

"In the morning, Germaine," said Ferdinand, with frigid courtesy, "we shall remove the court to Seville."

The Queen toyed idly with a quill and looked at her jewelled fingers. "It gives me little time for preparation," she replied calmly, "but if it is your wish, I can be ready."

"It is my wish!"

"But, after all, we have been at Burgos here for so short a time. I had thought of you as very happy here, Ferdinand." She smiled and pouted. "During the last year, we have removed so often that indeed it seems that we are in almost a perpetual state of migration."

"I tire easily of all places," said the King. "At the moment, I pine for Seville and the amusements there. This salt air begins to rack me."

"I have found it most invigorating. And yet,

your health is ever my first consideration. That, you know."

"I have never doubted it, Madame," replied the King politely. "Your own health is, however, less excellent than you think. Sometimes your hands are cold as ice, and again at times I feel them burn as with a fever. I have seen you shake as with an ague, when you did not know that my sympathetic gaze was upon you."

"I am very well," said the Queen, blushing.

"Permit me to be your adviser, in the absence of your physician," said the King.

"Very well! Seville, then, in the morning. I shall be ready."

"Good! And, by the way, our favourite, the handsome Perez de Ortubia, has been too long idle. So able a soldier must not be allowed to degenerate into a mere courtier. Do you not agree with me? We shall be sorry to lose him, of course, but he has qualities that peculiarly fit him for our service in the islands. I am directing that he return with our good Ponce, who shortly sails for Boriquen."

The Queen looked quickly up into the eyes that danced with malice. Then she bowed her head. "An excellent idea," she nodded, "although, as you say, we shall be sorry to see him go."

"Still, it is better for him than to be rotting here in Spain," continued the King. He left his seat and came gallantly to her side. "I am glad that, as usual, our ideas run in such close harmony." He proffered his arm. "May I not escort you to your chambers?"

Shortly thereafter, Juan Perez reported hastily to his new commander.

"On the morrow the court removes to Seville," he said. "I shall be back before we sail."

"If you will take an old man's advice, Juan Perez," replied the veteran bluntly, "you will remain with me at Burgos."

"But why?" cried Ortubia angrily, "What is it that you are suggesting?"

The commander shrugged. "Nothing," he said, "nothing at all. By all means go to Seville. You are a hothead and a fool. I shall not miss you greatly if you fail to return."

"I shall be with you a day before you sail," promised the courtier, and, remounting his horse, he rode rapidly to the palace. In the morning, he was an attractive part of the royal caravan, which in due time reached the city of Seville.

A question that particularly disturbed Ortubia, now that his career at court was run, was the matter of the vial that, ever and always, he carried

hidden upon his person. He was returning shortly
to the islands, where possibly the supply of youth
could in time be renewed. The King was obviously
dying by slow degrees; but the Queen was still
young and fair. Might it not be wise to whisper
the secret in her ear and give her the vial for her
preservation? Great God, she might use it to restore the King! Women were curious creatures,
whether they were queens or wenches. One never
knew what they would do next. Out of sight, out
of mind, was an old adage, and had been often
proved a true one. Yet, through the Queen, he—
Juan Perez de Ortubia—held the world in the
hollow of his hand. He held a secret that, upon the
death of Ferdinand, might carry him to such preferments as man never before had dreamed.

Turning the question in his mind, he decided
against immediate confession. There was still
plenty of time before he must sail. Better to save
the secret for an emergency. It might yet prove its
worth in some unimagined moment of stress.
The King unquestionably was suspicious; not,
however, of his subject's youth, but of his attach-
ment to Germaine. Still, one might suppose the
Queen able to take care of that situation. On the
whole, thought Juan Perez, it would be best to
say nothing for a time. And if the King should die

upon the morrow . . . at any time, indeed, before Juan Perez sailed . . .?

Germaine was less tranquil about the future. She witnessed the arrival of her lover with dismay, and at the first opportunity beseeched him to remove himself beyond danger. They stood together in a dim corner of the anteroom to her apartments in the palace at Seville, as twilight fell. Ortubia, clasping her in his arms, kissed her lips while she pleaded.

"Blind, blind!" she panted. "Can you not see why the court was removed from Burgos? It was to test you—and me! The King suspects. Had you remained behind upon the ships, all would have been well. You might have returned within a year —and I should have been waiting. Now you are here, and all his suspicions are confirmed. For God's sake, go quickly, Juan! Flee from me as if I were a pestilence. If we were taken in this position, nothing that I could do or say would save you. I am as powerless as one of my own pages, and as helpless."

He tightened his grasp upon her body, so that she bent backward in his embrace. Their lips clung wildly.

"Very well," he said, at length. "If it be your

wish, I shall go. I shall go at once. I can be mounted and away within an hour. I had hoped——"

"Hope for nothing!" she cried. "Every moment that passes increases your peril. It *is* my wish. Not that I willingly send you away from me. I love you! If I dared——"

Suddenly, with a scream, she tore herself from his arms, and flung up her hands before her face. There was a faint sound at the other side of the chamber, and in a moment a little tremor of the curtains, as if someone had passed through them, someone who had been listening within the room.

"A spy!" she gasped. "We have been over-heard."

Juan Perez ripped his sword from its sheath so that it hissed, and leaped to the door. He swung back the curtains and looked out into the corridor, now dim with evening. Then, quickly, he drew back, his heart between his lips. A long moment passed away, and again he peered out, cautiously this time, as a man in terror of his life.

Some distance along the corridor, a gaunt figure in black stood at a window and looked out into the gathering gloom. By the faint light that still entered and fell upon the man's face, Ortubia saw clearly the sneering features of the King of Spain.

A third time he looked, and the figure had vanished. He turned to speak with the Queen, but she had fled to her inmost chamber. With long strides, Juan Perez traversed the corridor and reached the courtyard. His horse was waiting. He laid a hand upon its crupper. A bold dash, now, and he might still reach the seacoast in time. . . . At the same instant, another hand was laid upon his shoulder, and Juan Perez knew that his high adventure was at an end.

A circle of armed soldiers surrounded him. He bowed to their leader and leaped into the saddle. "Which way, Captain?" he asked gaily, and, touching spurs to his animal, rode out of the courtyard with his escort.

For some miles they followed the beaten highway. No word was spoken. The moonlight fell upon helmet and cuirass, and upon the stern faces of his captors. The hoofs of the horses thudded in the road, and stirrup irons clinked in the darkness. Then, some distance beyond the city, the gray walls of a castle bulked above them, and lights gleamed upon the battlements. The company drew rein.

"What *is* this place, my captain?" asked the prisoner. "I do not seem to recall it."

"It is the fortress of Triana," answered the

officer; and at the words Juan Perez felt his face grow white. . . . He was in the hands of the Inquisition.

In his wildest imaginings of the fate that would be his, should the Queen's passion be discovered, this had not crossed his mind. He thought of the secret rooms beneath the fortress, of the deeds that went forward there, and his bowels became chambers of ice.

Thereafter, for a time, what happened was to Juan Perez only a fantastic nightmare, no detail of which stood forth clearly. Gates opened and closed behind him, lights flickered in dim corridors, and crooked stairways coiled downward into the earth. Before and behind him tramped grim figures in black robes, who spoke no word. A sense of dampness and cold stole over him; bolts grated and doors creaked in the silence, and at length a pallet of straw received his body. . . . When some hours had passed away, he knew that it was morning.

He stood, at length, before haggard priests in sable livery, and listened to the testimony of witnesses, as it was read to him. What charge would the King of Spain bring against his officer who had debauched the Queen's Majesty? Did the act constitute blasphemy, high treason, or conduct unbecoming an officer and a gentleman? And in

what wise could the Inquisition deal with it? He smiled a little, inwardly, and then was grave.

The charge was heresy. He was accused of the high crime of Judaism. In his veins, it was asserted, flowed the *mala sangre* of the house of Judah, that ignominious strain that no amount of breeding could purge away. His lips curled in a slow sneer. Yet why not? He could hardly be accused of the seduction of the Queen of Spain.

With keen interest, he listened to the presumptive proofs by which this more heinous sin was to be established.

Item, he had been seen to wear better clothing and cleaner linen on the Jewish sabbath.

Item, there had been no fire in his house on the evening preceding that holy day.

Item, he had sitten at table with a Jew and had eaten the meat of animals slaughtered by members of that race.

Item, he had been seen to drink a certain beverage held by the Jews in high esteem.

Item, once in camp, when he had thought himself to be dying, he had turned his face to the wall.

What had he to say for himself?

Juan Perez thought of the torture chamber, and the thought sickened him. There was no purer Castilian blood in the land than his own; but he realized that this was no ordinary prosecution. The King of Spain, himself, was behind it. Nothing that he could say could avail now to save him from his ultimate fate, already decided upon. Better to expedite it than to court the rack and pulley. An acquiescence might at least embarrass them. He shrugged and smiled.

"It is true, Holy Fathers," he replied suavely. "I am the vilest of Jews."

The Grand Inquisitor returned him an incredulous stare. "You admit it?" he demanded in astonishment. His malignant eyes gleamed through the eyeslits of his mask.

"Willingly, since it is true. It is my purpose to conceal nothing."

The inquisitors, stunned, conferred together in a corner.

"What have you to say in your defense?" they asked, at length.

Juan Perez, a sensible man who would instantly have turned Turk, if by so doing he might save his body from the fire, smiled blandly.

"What can one say?" he gestured. "Is it your wish that I recant and embrace the true faith of my country?"

"You are willing to recant?" screamed the inquisitor in chief, and turned helplessly to his coadjutors. It was embarrassing, certainly. The King's instructions had not contemplated such an attitude. They had been told that the prisoner would deny his race with fervour, to the end.

"Very willing," said Juan Perez truthfully. "For long, my convictions have been turning in that direction."

It was an unusual situation. Again the inquisitors drew apart and conferred earnestly together. A decision was reached.

"We suspect," said their spokesman darkly, "that your sudden conversion is one of convenience. We suspect that you are playing with this tribunal, which is of God, and with us, His ministers. If so, it shall be the worse for you. In the meantime, our judgment is deferred."

The Queen's lover was returned to his dungeon, where in darkness he awaited his fate. He had no delusions about it. He was marked for doom. His attitude before the Inquisition had saved him from preliminary torture, perhaps, but nothing more. The rack and pulleys he might have escaped, but the fagots were already cut that would light his passage to eternity.

Eternity! Once he had thought he held it in his hand. But with the destruction of his visible body, what was there to hope for? Was there an

eternity of life beyond the grave? And had he
sinned so grievously that it, too, would be denied
him? For a long time he pondered the situation.
His arms had been taken from him to prevent his
suicide, but curiously he had not otherwise been
searched. In the darkness he drew forth the vial
of water and touched it lovingly. Who, after his
death, would benefit by these precious drams?
Or would they perish with him? He had been foolish, perhaps, not to give the vial to Germaine,
when it was possible. To try to send it now would
be to lose it, without benefit to Germaine. If,
somehow, she could contrive to visit him in his
cell—— But such things happened only in legend.
He sighed, and knew that he had looked his last
upon the King's wife.

When some weeks had passed away, he began
to wonder if, by some miracle, he had been forgotten. Ponce, by this time, would have sailed. He
remembered his rash promise to the veteran, and
smiled forlornly. Was it possible to bribe the
guards? Only the vial remained wherewith to re-
ward a traitor. Still, it was worth thinking about.
He was still thinking about it, one evening, when
the door of his cell grated open and the dark forms
of his monkish captors appeared in the opening.
He rose painfully to his feet and followed them.

At the same instant, in the privacy of her boudoir, Germaine plucked a hand glass from an inlaid table, and laying her head back and to one side, looked at her image through half-closed lids. She was a lovely woman, although a queen, and this evening she was alone. The King was mysteriously absent from the palace; her maids had been dismissed. She smiled and dimpled roguishly at her reflection, raising a languid hand to push back her hair at the temples. And then the mirror darkened, and in its depths another face appeared, as if within a crystal. She gasped, then cried out happily, and, turning, leaned to the embrace of the young courtier who smiled upon her.

"Francisco," she breathed. He lowered his handsome head and murmured her name against her cloudy hair.

Juan Perez de Ortubia, stumbling through gloomy corridors in the wake of a dancing light, murmured the same name in the silence, and found a curious comfort thereby.

He had been wrong about Juan Ponce, however. The old commander had not yet sailed, for the reason that he had as yet received neither his appointments nor his sailing orders. The King had forgotten Juan Ponce, not Juan Perez. Wherefore, that veteran, upon a day, mounted a borrowed steed and rode heavily after his dilatory monarch.

Arriving in Seville, toward evening he demanded audience with Ferdinand; but the King had disappeared. None knew what had become of him. Angrily, the fat knight trod the thoroughfares, communing with himself, and in time his aimless feet, following those of a howling mob, led him to a central square in the suburbs of the city. With a start, he realized his surroundings.

On all sides of the cleared space, the mob struggled and murmured, some hissing and some cheering. In the centre, a spacious stone scaffold rose upward, with the blank-eyed figures of four prophets at its corners. It was, as the worthy curate of Los Palacios later described it, the spot where heretics were burned, and ought to burn as long as any could be found.

A dreadful fascination held Juan Ponce to the scene. The murmur of the crowd welled higher in the night, and he glanced quickly toward the steps that led upward to the scaffold. A party of men was slowly making its way to the platform. They were black-robed monks, bearing aloft the banners of the Holy Office. In their midst walked a tall man in a coarse woollen garment that rose closely around his neck and dropped like a frock to his knees. The garment was of yellow cloth, embroidered with a scarlet cross, and was further embellished with the figures of devils and coiling tongues of flame, as suggesting the victim's destiny.

The man walked proudly and with a certain arrogance that appealed to the veteran. He walked like a soldier. There was something indeed curiously familiar about his head and gait. Then a torch flare fell for an instant upon his features. God in Heaven! It was Perez de Ortubia! They were tying him to one of the stone figures of the scaffold.

Juan Ponce's rancour fell away from him as if it had never been. For a moment, he writhed forward in the press, with some wild thought of rescue. Then he stopped and turned back. There was nothing now that he could do for Juan Perez de Ortubia, save perhaps to burn candles for his soul. Any recklessness now would but serve to turn the King's anger upon himself.

As he struggled back to the outskirts of the horde, he heard the sudden hiss and crackle of burning fagots and smelled the smoke of dry wood burning. A deep roar went up from the mob, in which were mingled anathema and applause. Men shrieked and whistled, and women danced together with nameless emotions.

At the edge of the crowd, as the veteran at

length fought free, a gaunt figure flitted across his vision, a man in the black cloak and bonnet of the peasants of Aragon. His face was contorted with triumph and hatred; his eyes flamed with demoniac lights. He tossed his arms skyward and shouted as if in ecstasy. For a fleeting instant, in the poor light, Juan Ponce saw the madman's face. It was the face of Ferdinand of Spain.

The veteran turned and fled. Thank God, there were still undiscovered islands in the sea!

BOOK TWO

CHAPTER SIX

IN WHICH A GENTLEMAN OF GOD SUFFERS SOME EMBARRASSMENT

It is evident, my boy, that a man without breeches is in a state highly inconvenient to speak of sacred truth, to confound error and to prevent crime.
—ANATOLE FRANCE.

It will soon be quite three hundred years since the obscure Spanish priest, Mendez, came up to Rome from his little parish of Calaveras, with a special purpose in mind. His idea was to gain the ear of the Christian world to certain theological views, then peculiar to himself. Although obscure, Mendez had the good fortune to be a friend of the Cardinal Secretary of State, a circumstance that was worth to him at least a lodging in the Vatican.

Good Father Mendez, although verging upon seventy, was still vigorous of mind if frail of body. He was, moreover, possessed with the idea that the world could not very well get on without the aid of the treatise on theology with which he was armed, but for the printing of which he had failed to obtain the necessary permission of the Master of the Sacred Palace. Wherefore, to accomplish his benevolent purpose without the required license, the excellent priest procured type and a printing press, and caused them to be conveyed to his apartment, which chanced to be over that occupied by the Master of the Sacred Palace. This was an error, for when he set his press to work, the noise it made was so unusual that it quickly attracted attention. The offense was detected and reported to the Pope's Holiness, from whom issued immediate orders for Mendez and his theology to quit Rome.

Assuming, however, that nothing more would be heard of the press or its proprietor, the Cardinal Secretary of State did not push the execution of the Pope's orders. Mendez, safely removed from his dangerous quarters, found domicile elsewhere in the Eternal City and resumed his labours.

While thus lingering at sufferance in Rome, and on one of the hottest days of August in the year of grace called 1549, the reckless priest, glancing from his window, beheld a squad of the pontifical police taking possession of his doorway. He not unnaturally hurried to the conclusion that they were in quest of himself.

Although at the moment stripped to his shirt and drawers, the good man had such a wholesome dread of a Roman prison, that, without pausing to perfect his toilet, he fled up the stairs, crawled out upon the roof, and sought refuge in the first opening in the housetops that offered him a chance for concealment.

By the most astonishing good fortune, it proved to conduct to the interior of a convent of Magdalenes, a sort of closed establishment appropriated to the seclusion of women of equivocal characters, *donne male maritate*. And it so happened that among the recent additions to this frail circle was a damsel of considerable beauty, with whom Mendez had some slight acquaintance. She was, in point of fact, from his own parish in Calaveras, where her parents were known as devout and God-fearing citizens.

The inmates of the house, seeing a man descend among them in such guise, took it for granted that it was the *bellissima* who had attracted him. For a time the dovecote was violently fluttered. Whether impelled by jealousy or consternation, someone at last rang the bell of the convent, and in a moment the embarrassed Mendez, in his hasty toilet, was surrounded by a throng of curious and indignant women. In their midst was the *bellissima*, whom he instantly recognized.

"Is it you, Rafaela?" he asked eagerly, pressing

his ancient knees tightly together. "See, it is I, Father Mendez, your father's friend! Tell them that I am quite harmless. They will not listen. I swear to you that it was an accident."

For an instant, a smile tugged at the corners of the scarlet mouth; then the girl's face became grave. She glanced quickly at the nun in charge and ventured timidly: "Indeed, Sister Beatrice, it is as Father Mendez says. I did not at first recognize him, and there is nothing to wonder at in that; but he is a good man and would not come here except by an accident."

"An accident!" snorted the nun, glancing suspiciously from one of them to the other, as if associating the man and her charge in a conspiracy. "What sort of an accident, I should like to know, would send a man parading on the rooftops without clothing? Was this his custom in Calaveras, when he was your father's friend? Was it his habit to drop in upon your father from the roof, clad only in his undergarments?"

"My dear sister!" protested the old priest, horrified and ready to collapse from mortification. "Let me explain. I assure you I can explain."

"I shall be glad to hear your explanation," said the nun frigidly. To the surrounding women she cried: "Be off with you, you shameless hussies, to your devotions and to your tasks. All of you, save only Rafaela. I shall investigate this vulgarity myself."

With mingled emotions, the Magdalenes dispersed, leaving the priest blushing between the two women, one old and hard, the other young and tender.

The glance of the older woman softened when she had heard the story. "What is the nature of your contribution to theology?" she asked.

"Dear sister," cried Father Mendez, "have you no wrap that I may throw about me first? I am ready to die of shame at the humiliation I have brought upon us all."

"Nay, Father," said the nun. "Since there was no offense intended, there shall be none taken. Take no shame for the accident. You shall have one of the *bellissima*'s robes to throw about you. See to it, Rafaela." And as the girl departed, she continued: "What you have told me of your ideas interests me deeply, Father."

"But I have told you nothing as yet, my sister. In brief, 'tis this: that the soul of man is the temple and the abode of God, which therefore we should be careful to keep as clean and pure as possible from worldliness and the lusts of the flesh; from all the prides of life."

"How true that is!" cried Sister Beatrice. "I cannot understand, Father, how such a doctrine could operate only to bring about your arrest."

"Nor·I! I am sure that there is some error, which in time will be corrected. I shall be happy, Sister, to give you a copy of my pamphlet, when I have opportunity to return to my lodging. You will like it, I am sure. In it, I set forth that the true end of human life ought to be, as far as possible, the attainment of perfection. In the progress toward this result, I distinguish two principal stages or degrees, the first attainable by meditation, the second and highest by contemplation. In the first stage, the attention is fixed upon the capital truths of religion, upon all the circumstances under which religion has been commended to us; objections are wrestled with, and doubts which might trouble the soul, one by one are resolved and banished. In this stage, it is the reason that acts, mainly, and often in opposition to the natural man. And one does not reach the higher stage of devotion until the soul has ceased to struggle, until it has no further need of proofs or reflection, until it contemplates the truth in silence and repose. This is what is termed retirement of the soul and perfect contemplation, in which the soul does not reason nor reflect, neither about God nor itself, but passively receives the impressions of celestial light, undisturbed by the world or its works."

At this moment the *bellissima* returned with a long garment for her father's friend, who seized it and flung it from him in an ecstasy.

"Whenever the soul can be lifted up to this state," he continued eagerly, "it desires nothing, not even its own salvation; it fears nothing, not even the torments of hell. It becomes indifferent to the use of sacraments and to all the practices of sensible devotion, having transcended the sphere of their efficacy."

"Ah!" cried Sister Beatrice, while Rafaela stared, speechless, at the wrinkled raiment of the priest, "there, I fear, is where the Holy Father differs with you. For if our external acts of devotion are to be slighted, and transgressors are to go directly to their Maker with their budget of sins, however grievous; if they are never to leave their rooms to ask intercession for the deliverance of souls from Purgatory, what is to become of our Church? How is it to be supported? What is to become of the Confessional?"

"It is a practical aspect that has nothing of holiness to recommend it," said Father Mendez impatiently. "The Divine Majesty knows very well that it is not by the means of one's own ratiocination or industry that a soul draws near to Him and understands the divine truths, but rather by a silent and humble resignation. What an instance of this did the Patriarch Noah give, who, after he had been by all men reckoned a fool, floating in the middle of a raging sea wherewith the world was overflowed, without sails or oars and environed by ferocious beasts, walked by faith alone, not knowing or understanding what God in His wisdom had a mind to do with him!"

He tossed his arms toward the ceiling. "It concerns us only, my sister," he cried, "to prepare our hearts like clean paper whereon the Divine Wisdom may imprint characters to His own liking."

"Here is the robe, Holy Father," said the *bellissima* shyly, and held forth the rejected garment.

Remembering his all but primitive condition, Father Mendez blushed painfully and snatched the robe about him. "At least, dear sister," he stammered, "and you, my good Rafaela, I have convinced you that my entrance upon your privacy was not by calculation prejudicial to yourselves."

"What you have told us has been most interesting," said the older woman. "Your visit has been most inspiring. I should be happy to hear more of these doctrines of yours, Father, so strange and new and yet so quieting."

"And I, at any time, would be happy to instruct you further."

"Since you have come among us, however strangely," continued the nun, dropping her eyes, "I cannot send you away to possible imprisonment. You have, in effect, asked sanctuary of us. Are you not afraid to return to your lodging, Father?"

"I dread it greatly," said Father Mendez.

"Stay with us, then, until such time as you may safely venture forth. Here, none will think to look for you; and we shall be lifted up by your presence. There is a room, separated from our own quarters, that you might occupy without discomfort."

"Thank you, my dear sister, for your understanding and for your mercy. And you, Rafaela, save for whose introduction my intentions had been misunderstood."

Walking awkwardly in his borrowed robe, he allowed himself to be conducted to his chamber.

But, in the morning, good Father Mendez, who had slept but ill, what with his worries and the strangeness of his bedchamber, thanked his benefactors for their protection and declined further to incriminate them.

"I should not wish to draw suspicion upon you,

dear sister," he said, "nor upon these repentant children who, by God's grace, have been won back to righteousness. The very nature of their previous error too readily allows the uncharitable to asperse the sincerity of their repentance. Were it known that a man had spent the night within your walls, even I, a priest of God, I shudder to think what slanderous tongues might whisper. My problem is my Maker's and my own. By your leave, however, I must continue to wear this robe, which you have lent me, until such time as I may resume my own garments."

Saying which, he blessed them all and, followed by their good wishes, ascended to the upper story and climbed out upon the roof. The comparative coolness of early morning refreshed him, and advancing quickly to his own opening, he cautiously descended to his lodging. To his surprise, all was as he had left it. His papers, his printing press, and his pamphlets were untouched.

Was it a trick? he wondered. Were there, perhaps, emissaries of the papal police loitering near to catch him in the act of flight? He glanced suspiciously from his window, but there was no one within view. His doorway was empty. Slowly, he crept down the stairs, and encountered no one upon his way. Escape lay before him, if he had but the courage to act quickly. In time, the police would return, and he would be haled with all his writings to a Roman prison. Turning, he fled upward to his room and began to collect his belongings. He would go back to Spain, back to his own land and his own parish, where his simple views were not regarded as of the world and the flesh.

In half an hour, all was ready. His printing press he would have to leave, but his books and papers, in a great bundle, were not too heavy for his years. Beneath his arm he carried a smaller packet in which were the few valuables that he still possessed tied neatly in an extra cassock. Once more he descended the steps and peered cautiously into the street. It was still empty of human life. The sun was beginning to give promise of another day of extreme heat; birds were singing in the trees near at hand; a gaunt cat, threadbare and unhappy, slunk across the road and into an alley. A vendor of milk was banging his bottles in the next block. Clasping his great bundle tightly, Father Mendez stepped out of his doorway and walked rapidly away. As he progressed, he turned his head over his shoulder, now and then, to be sure that he was not followed.

At the first intersection of highways, he increased his pace, and turning at the same instant to look backward, crashed heavily into a hurrying stranger in the other street.

Before the onslaught of the human ram the old priest went down upon the walk; his bundle escaped his grasp and burst, scattering his books and papers in every direction. He tried to rise and resume his flight, but a stabbing pain in his ankle told him that he was hurt. With a gasp of resignation and a muttered prayer, he sank back upon the pavement. In a moment, however, the stranger's arm was around his shoulderblades and he was being hoisted to his feet. Swaying unsteadily, he looked at the man who had brought about his downfall.

"Well, well," cried the stranger, with rough sympathy, "I beg your pardon, Father, I'm sure. I did not see you, and I'm afraid you didn't see me. I suspect that we were both of us woolgathering. Are you hurt?"

He was a tall man of middle age, with a flashing, humorous eye and a peaked red beard; a heavy man, strongly builded and vigorous, attired in sober garments of excellent cut and material. It seemed to Father Mendez that never had he seen so bright and kindly an eye in human features. Instinctively, his trust went out to this stranger.

"I think I have twisted my ankle," said the priest, trying to stand upon it.

"*Tiens!* but I am sorry. Let me help you. Sit down here against this house for a moment while I gather up your books and papers. You are a scholar, I see, although a priest. They are not always to be found in the same cassock. It is always a pleasure to meet a scholar; but, believe me, it is not my habit to knock down all I meet." As he spoke, smiling whimsically at his victim, he brought back the scattered papers and piled them neatly before their author. "There, that is all, I think. Where were you headed, Father? Since you walk with difficulty and I have no horse, it is only fair for me to assist you with my arm."

It occurred suddenly to Father Mendez that he did not know where he was headed, except, ultimately, for Spain. He said as much.

"Well," laughed the good-humoured stranger, "you are still some miles from Spain, as doubtless you know. There is quite a jaunt ahead of you, if you plan to walk it. Since I am myself a native of France, I am also a stranger in a strange land— and, God knows, it grows stranger the longer I know it. I am a physician and at your service. My lodging is not far. Come, lean upon me as we walk, and in a few minutes I shall make you feel more at ease."

"You are very good," said the priest gratefully. "You were sent to me by Heaven."

"Not a doubt of it," said the physician, "although the violence of my greeting might suggest an alternative to you. I am pleased to tell you that all the folks were well and happy there, when I came away—although somewhat concerned about the confusion and stupidity that flourish hereabouts. Your great-aunt Ida sent her love. Does your ankle bother you greatly?"

Startled by his companion's speech, the old priest had stopped. Now he went on. "It is a little stronger, thank you," he replied.

"It was certainly fortuitous that, since you chose to be knocked down to-day, you selected a physician when you brought about the collision," continued the irrepressible stranger. "I am supposed to be quite good at my profession, although it brings me little enough. Not that it matters really! I assure you that half the existing population of earth might perish of the plague or pox, for all of me. Half? Nine tenths would be closer to the mark. But I would except the worthy scholars, such as ourselves, even if they were priests." He chuckled merrily. "Don't you ever feel like running amuck, Father, and massacring whole villages?"

"Why—why," stammered Father Mendez, dismayed, "I cannot say that any such idea ever has occurred to me, my dear sir! Why should they be massacred?"

"Oh, for anything or for nothing. Principally because they would then be dead. The world is filled with very stupid swine, you know."

"Their lives were given them by God," said Father Mendez virtuously.

"Yes, yes, but so were their brains, which they are so careful not to exercise. Yet if one should exercise his body to make it stronger and finer, should not one similarly exercise his brain to the same end?" The hearty physician smiled quaintly and showed his strong white teeth. He playfully pinched the lean arm that lay within his own. "What would you say," he asked, "if I were tell to you that I, too, had worn the cloth?"

"You!" cried the old man, astounded and horrified. "You—a priest!"

"Why not? What is there strange about that?"

Father Mendez temporized. "You do not—your speech, I should say, is not exactly that of a priest of God—or so it seemed to me." He was deeply dismayed. "Did you not say that you were a physician?"

"Ah, I reformed! I rapidly discovered that I had

mistaken my calling, and rather than perpetuate an error, I corrected it. I am now a physician. To be honest with you, I should be a famous poet, if I could. However, I'm not complaining. Every man to his taste, as the farmer said when he kissed the cow. Did you ever hear the story of the doctor who was called to minister to a lady's maid? It's one of the best!"

"I am afraid—afraid that I have not heard it," stammered Father Mendez.

"You'll love it! This maid, it seems, had taken to her bed, pretending illness, apparently to get out of her tasks. Her mistress, a vinegary bitch, suspected the imposture, and to show the girl up, sent for a physician. Well, he came and looked her over—the girl, you understand, not the mistress. There was no doubt of it; she was pretending. So as soon as the lady had left the room, the physician turned to the maid and accused her. 'Get up,' he said. 'Get up and put on your clothes! You can't fool me.'"

He continued to the end, finishing with a shout of laughter that froze the priest's blood in his veins. But before a protest could be entered, they had reached the lodging of the boisterous physician, and Father Mendez was being urged up the staircase.

"Permit me," said the doctor, placing his charge in a chair; and, stooping, he deftly removed the priest's shoes and stockings and attentively examined both feet. "So!" he continued soothingly. "You'll be all right, now, in a little while. I'm merely going to get some warm water. Meanwhile, permit me to introduce myself: François Rabelais, bachelor of medicine, of Chinon, in the country of France."

"I am Peter Mendez," said the priest, "of Calaveras, in Aragon."

"Good! You shall tell me all your troubles presently. Everybody likes to tell his troubles to a physician." He bustled away to prepare his bandages and water.

Father Mendez was, in fact, very glad to tell his troubles to so sympathetic an audience; and in the days that followed his introduction into the physician's rooms, he decided that, for all of his new friend's exuberant spirits and nerve-shaking humour, François Rabelais was a man of sense and penetration. The physician even listened with approval to the theology of Peter Mendez, and pronounced it superior to any other then in vogue.

"An admirable idea!" cried Rabelais, when he heard the treatise. "It abolishes the Confessional with all its perquisites, and if carried to its ultimate, it will abolish the Church, a consummation devoutly to be desired. But you are in for trouble, Father, if you press it. Take my word for it. I have myself courted disaster a number of times, by disturbing the serenity of Mother Church! I am even now somewhat suspect. You are not acquainted, I take it, with my own small contributions to theology? I feared as much. But you shall see them. I shall present you with copies of each, which afterward, if you do not like them, you may use for shaving paper."

"How are they called, these books?" asked Mendez eagerly.

"The first I called—after its central character—*Gargantua;* it is a giant-story of great humour and penetration, although the critics have damned it. It made me so much trouble that, a few years later, I published a sequel to it, which I called *Pantagruel* —a joyous chronicle that you will be sure to like; it is so full of—of—pantagruelism. By the Mass, Father, your own little adventure with the soiled doves is a gem. I regret that it comes to me so late. If again I become an author, you are like to find yourself celebrated."

Father Mendez was shocked. "I beg of you to do nothing of the sort," he pleaded. "Already I am more conspicuous a character than is to my taste.

I ask nothing more than to return safely to my own village."

"Of course," continued the scandalous physician, "you would have to make love to the good sister in charge, and thereby win her to your fell purposes with reference to her protégés. What was the number of them, did you say? Faith, what a tale 'twould make! How long do you suppose it would take a man, reasonably vigorous, to work his way through such a seminary? Well, well, be of good cheer! I shall do no more than tell the tale as it should have happened, and for those who will appreciate it. I am done with authorship and its rewards. The devil take it!"

To all of this Father Mendez listened with terror, while waiting for the blast from the clouds that would strike them both to earth. In time, he came to know that his protector was only frightening him with words. In his heart, he liked the apostate monk of Chinon, who railed at church and clergy, life and death, with sardonic impartiality, yet practised his humane profession with zeal and piety.

When a fortnight had gone over his head, and still he lingered with the physician, there occurred an incident that laid his last doubt as to the fine humanity of Master François Rabelais.

Waking somewhat earlier than was his wont, on a morning in early September, Father Mendez was amazed to hear in the room beyond his chamber the sound of voices in amiable discourse. One voice was that of Dr. Rabelais, his benefactor; but the other . . . ? It was the voice of a woman, and somewhere he had heard it before. In a moment it came to him. *Rafaela!* The little Magdalene of the convent, the *bellissima* whose father he had shriven! What could she be doing in the bedchamber of his friend?

After a moment, he smiled. She had sought *him* out, of course, her old confessor, and was but awaiting the hour of his rising. His heart, which for an instant had stopped beating, ticked on. He smiled again, happily.

"I am awake, Rafaela!" he called. "In just a moment, I shall join you."

An exclamation of surprise and apprehension sounded in the next apartment. Then the voices became low and urgent, the words indistinguishable one from another. Master Rabelais was explaining.

Hastily throwing on his robe and plucking another from its nail, the priest strode into the outer chamber.

The physician, wrapped to his bare heels in a

blanket, was seated on the foot of a small bed beneath the covers of which, drawn upward to her chin, curved the slender body of the young girl. Good Father Mendez beamed upon them both.

"Rafaela," he said, "I am sorry that I was not up to receive you. Here is your robe, my dear, which I have kept safely for you, and for which I thank you. How you have sought me out, I cannot guess; but tell me quickly: are you in trouble?"

"Nay, Father," she answered, abashed, and stole a glance at the physician. "When I came here to seek you, you were not yet arisen, and this kind gentleman was so good as to befriend me. I was ill and wished your counsel and assistance."

"You were ill? And did they not attend you at the convent?"

Her eyelids were lowered before his gaze. "In truth, Father, I ran away from the convent, not long after you were there. The food was dreadful and the life confining. Then I fell ill, and last night, while seeking *you*, I had the good fortune to accost this gentleman, who told me that you were here. Was it not a strange coincidence?"

As she did not quite tell the truth about her reason for accosting the physician, her father's friend did not realize how extraordinary the coincidence had been.

"Amazing!" agreed the priest, with grateful emphasis. "Thus, twice, my brother, have you been an instrument of grace. It is in such strange and significant incidents that God makes His mercies known."

"I was astounded when Rafaela informed me that it was you whom she sought," testified François Rabelais devoutly.

"No more than I to learn that he was here with you," cried Rafaela. Her surprise was, indeed, so fresh that it was still upon her and lent conviction to her words.

"We must take counsel together," said Father Mendez, "and decide what is to become of you, Rafaela. Perhaps it would be well if you were to return with me to Calaveras."

"Quite so," agreed the physician briskly. "Something should be done, as you rightly observe. The more so, Father, as I find that shortly I must return to France. The Cardinal du Bellay, in whose service I act as secretary, has been superseded, I grieve to say, and we depart within a few days." He wrapped his blanket more closely about him, and smiled paternally upon the girl.

Father Mendez was overcome. "How I at first misjudged you!" he cried. "And now to find that you are in the service of that distinguished prelate!"

"An excellent fellow, too," commented Rabelais. "With reference to Rafaela, however, I have already told her that I shall be glad to recommend her to some friends of mine in the city, who I am sure will find her in all ways as sweet and delightful as have I. It will relieve your mind about her, Father, and I am sure they will make her happy. She sends her great love to her mother, and these gold pieces, which I am happy to hand to you." He seized a purse from the table, with a quick gesture, and recklessly extracted some of its contents.

"God has been kind to you, Rafaela," said the priest almost sternly, as he accepted the money. "You should never cease to thank Him for this day."

"An incredible episode indeed," declared Rabelais. "Were I to add that chapter I spoke of to my giant-story, with this new conclusion, I vow there would be none to believe it."

Thus it fell out that, when the sun had risen less than an hour, Rafaela slipped quietly from the house, and, with the blessing of Father Mendez, tripped quickly away upon her new employment, which was in point of fact neither new nor old, but a little of both. And, at the same time, she trips daintily out of the narrative, since no further record of her ever has been found.

When she had been gone for about an hour, Father Mendez, untying his spare cassock and turning over the valuables that he possessed, picked out of the pathetic heap a jewelled vial of slender length and graceful design, the stopper of which had been sealed into place with red wax. Then, seeking through his sheaves of papers, he extracted a parchment manuscript and went in search of his friend. The vial he carried between his thumb and fingers, and at some distance from his body, as if it were filled with some deadly poison or explosive. In this wise, he came upon the physician in his study.

"My brother," said Father Mendez humbly, "there is nothing that I can give you in appreciation save only this vial. Read first this paper that I hand you, which is in Latin, and tell me then whether you will accept it."

With a surprised glance at the gleaming vial, Master Rabelais took the parchment and read what it contained.

I, Dominic Oviedo, of the Order of Saint Dominic, bequeath this vial to him who shall have the courage to employ it. It is of the Devil, I make no doubt; yet it was given me as the veritable waters of the fabled fountain of Bimini, which it is written are of such marvellous virtue that being drunk (perhaps with some diet) make old men young again. And here I must make protestation not to think this to be said lightly or rashly, for they have so spread this rumour for a truth throughout all the world, that not only all the people, but many of them whom wisdom or fortune has divided from the common sort, think it to be true. This vial, said to contain the waters of this famous spring, three drops of which are said to be sufficient to insure immortality for him who shall drink, were given to me, Dominic Oviedo, by one Perez de Ortubia, a prisoner of the Holy Inquisition, in this year of Our Lord, fifteen hundred and fourteen, who by the gift sought to seduce me from my vows, praying that I would aid him to escape. It was his assertion that he had with his own hands filled the vial at the fountain of youth, the history of whose search is as follows. The Governor of Boriquena, Juan Ponce de León, being discharged of his office and very rich, furnished and sent forth two caravels to seek the Island of Boynca or Bimini, in which the Indians affirmed to be this running spring of youth. But while he travelled six months with outrageous desire among many islands to find what he sought, and could find no token of any such fountain, Perez de Ortubia, his captain, unknown to his great commander, came upon the fountain alone and drank of the waters, of which later he filled this vial. That they were of no virtue to aid him from the flames can be testified by me, who saw him perish."

Without comment, but with astonishment in every line of his face, the physician reached for the glittering container. His eyes were wide, and a little smile hovered remotely about his lips. Turning the gleaming toy in his long fingers, he surveyed it with comic dismay and not without admiration.

"Good God!" he exploded, at length. "Excuse me, but where, Father, did you get this thing?"

Father Mendez seated himself slowly, and for a moment his fists were pressed fiercely against his eyes. After a time he looked up.

"I will tell you all about it," he answered. "In the year 1514, my brother, you must know that I was in the city of Seville—an agent of the Inquisition. I was young and fiery, no more than thirty-five years of age. I am seventy now, an old man. Since that day, I have learned tolerance and kindness. . . . There was brought before the Inquisition, a young cavalier of Spain; he who is mentioned in that paper—Juan Perez de Ortubia. He was accused of heresy; but the real charge against him was never mentioned. He was the Queen's lover. And so he had to die. Father Dominic Oviedo was his jailer, and Ortubia sought to corrupt him, as the paper states; but Father Dominic Oviedo betrayed his prisoner. He accepted the vial and allowed Ortubia to perish."

For a few moments, he was silent, while Rabelais awaited patiently the conclusion.

"Whether it was an act of God, I cannot say, but, in a short time thereafter, Father Dominic Oviedo sickened and died. I was his confessor at the last. I had not seen Ortubia perish. I knew nothing about this vial. On his deathbed, Father Dominic gave it to me, with this paper. I have kept them ever since."

The physician leaned forward with an incredulous frown. "You have never tasted of the waters?" he asked.

"Never! Nor have I any wish to taste them. It was I who sealed the vial at its mouth. I agree with Father Dominic Oviedo that they are most likely of the Devil. Yet something has prevented me from destroying them, as it prevented Father Dominic. Hoping for greater wisdom, I kept them. Now I would not use them if I knew them to be potent to preserve me to the end of this earth. I have been near to a prison within these last few weeks, and I fled in terror, but not because I feared death. It is life that I fear. I may yet die in a prison. If so, I shall thank God that I am mortal and can die."

François Rabelais, bachelor of medicine, rose quickly to his feet and bowed to this philosophy. He seized the priest's hand in a warm clasp.

"Thank you," he said, "for your words and for

your generous gift. I shall treasure both. What
may be the meaning of this curiosity, theological
or scientific, I have no idea. It may be utter nonsense, some hoax of this man Ortubia's. Or it
may be—who knows what?"

"To-morrow," said the priest, "I shall resume
my journey toward Spain. We shall not meet
again on this earth. Again I thank you, for Rafaela
and for myself."

Master Rabelais had the grace to blush.

"Heaven protect you, Peter Mendez," he said.
"You are a good man."

But when the priest had been some three days
and nights upon his way, François Rabelais
reached a decision. For three nights he had studied
the manuscript of Dominic Oviedo, and for three
nights he had turned the vial in his hands and
picked tentatively at the withholding wax.

"Why not?" he asked, at length, aloud. "If it
is poison, I shall detect it. If it is mere water, it
will do me no harm. And if, by some stupendous
miracle, it should be . . . !"

With the point of his knife he snapped the wax
seals and extracted the stopper. He tested a single
drop upon his finger, sniffing and tasting it critically. It was undoubtedly water that the vial contained. Only water. Yet three drops, the will of

Dominic Oviedo had said, would make a man immortal. With a queer smile, Rabelais tilted the vial to his lips.

It was the merest water. . . .

And yet . . . did he only imagine that his blood had quickened? That his pulse beat more strongly was no cause for excitement; it might be attributed to the state of nerves into which he had worked himself over this absurd business. And yet . . .

He rose to his feet at a bound, and fire and honey seemed to throb and riot in his veins. A gay and ribald ballad rose quickly to his lips. He wondered where Rafaela had gone and whether she might be found again.

He melted some wax—green this time—and again sealed the stopper into the vial's throat. With a sharp little tool, he engraved some words upon the golden setting of the glass, and smiled at his handiwork. Vial and parchment he put away in his private cabinet. Then, whistling, he went out into the streets.

Exactly when or how Dr. François Rabelais lost the vial of youth is not certain, but it is on record that he undertook its recovery, since he has himself written, in an addition to his giant-stories, of his search for the Holy Bottle. There is a tradition that he died in his own country, in the year of his

Lord, fifteen hundred and fifty-three, and that his enemies rejoiced. It is tradition only. Unless he has been knifed, or burned, or blown to pieces by a cannon, it is quite possible that François Rabelais is living yet.

CHAPTER SEVEN

IN WHICH SWORDS RATTLE AND A WOMAN SCREAMS

Ah! . . . Paris wrapped in night! half nebulous:
The moonlight streams o'er the blue-shadowed roofs;
A lovely frame for this wild battle-scene;
Beneath the vapour's floating scarves, the Seine
Trembles, mysterious, like a magic mirror,
And, shortly, you shall see what you shall see!
                            —EDMOND ROSTAND.

Thus it was, and that which follows is as extraordinary as that which has gone before. Ah, a mad world, my masters!

Near the village of Jammes, which is in France and not too far from the outskirts of Paris, in the years between—let us say—1640 and 1659, there flourished an inn or *auberge* of no great repute or consequence. It was known as the Red Rooster, or perhaps the Gray Goose, such being the curious names fancied by the proprietors of inns in those days. And it was a spot not unknown to the brawling musketeers of King Louis, and to the no less brawling gentlemen of the Cardinal's Guard; while there came also to its dubious doors, thieves, men-

dicants, abductors, seducers, priests, harlots, no-
bles, and scoundrels of every kind.

Upon a particular evening of one of these un-
specified years, a night of storm and wind, there
sat beside a deal table in the common hall, a for-
midable-looking gentleman in the uniform of one
of the military outfits of the period. Fierce of eye
and haughty of demeanour, he would have been a
handsome man had it not been for his enormous
nose, which was so long, and withal so grotesque,
as almost to warrant the name of proboscis. His
long sword and cloak lay across the table beside
him, what time he toyed idly with a leathern cup,
spilling from time to time its contents across the
boards of the table. These were bits of bone, and
when he had spilled them, he recaptured all with
a swift movement, and repeated the performance,
cursing melodiously when his throw was bad and
smiling when it was good. At his left elbow stood
a number of bottles and a tall flagon, and at the
far end of the low chamber, a young pullet turned
with many savoury twistings upon a spit before the
open fire. The soldier, an officer by his facings, was
quite alone, save for the landlord who perspired
before the spit, and a kitchen wench, invisible, who
rattled pots in an adjoining room. Now and then,
in the intervals of his dicing, the soldier paused to

stroke his prodigious nose and to frown at the closed door leading into the night.

Outside, the storm was increasing. Dark clouds obscured the heavens, concealing moon and stars, which shone, no doubt, somewhere beyond the immediate turmoil. The flashes of lightning that gleamed along the horizon showed a white and solitary road, swept bare of travellers. As the storm gathered volume, these flashes succeeded one another with greater frequency and deep-toned thunder rolled across the sky. The wind whistled sharply at the shutters.

At his table, the officer with the Nose continued to rattle his dice, but at every new sound from without he glanced quickly toward the door, as if expecting it to fly open before the advent of another guest. When the pullet was ready for serving, it was placed before him. But although its odours caused the great nose to twitch and a smile to wreathe the bearded lips, he still glanced anxiously toward the closed door and ceaselessly rattled his dice.

"Your friend is long in coming, Chevalier," ventured the host, as he set down the steaming fowl and prepared to depart. His glance was that of a dog that was willing to be friendly but expected to be kicked.

Twisting his long moustaches, tinged with gray, the officer looked up. "He is overdue," he admitted, "but he will come. When he comes, he will be able to verify my suspicion that this wine of yours is not of the best. He has the finest taste and the noblest thirst in France."

With a sob, the landlord snatched one of the impugned bottles from the table and kissed it passionately. "It is the rarest wine in all the country round," he asserted; and he called upon Heaven to hear him and witness his assertion.

"We shall see," nodded the soldier carelessly. "Meanwhile, as the supply is running low, order me up another dozen from the cellars."

Bowing humbly, the man departed upon his errand, while the officer looked hungrily at the pullet, weltering in its grease. "I vow," said he, addressing the bird before him, "were it anyone but D'Artagnan, I should refuse to wait another minute!"

At the same instant, over the downpour of the rain and the clacking of the shutters, his ear caught the sound of hoofs in the road. They came nearer and stopped at length before the door. Then the door burst inward, and a man entered with a shout, a tall figure in an horseman's cloak. He was steaming wet, and his plume dripped soggily into his bosom.

"Cyrano!" cried the newcomer, at sight of the officer's nose. "A thousand pardons, *mon ami*, for my tardiness." He flung his wet wrappings upon a bench and rushed forward to embrace his friend.

"I am glad to see you," smiled the other, "but you were just in time. In another moment, I swear I should have begun upon the pullet."

"I was detained," said the cavalier called D'Artagnan, who wore the uniform of a captain of musketeers. "These cursed roads are almost impassable. We have swum nearly all the way from Paris. Boil me, but I am hungry—and thirsty, too! Say not another word until we have finished, if you love me. I could eat a bullock. But where is our sad-faced host?" And suddenly he began to bellow like the animal he had mentioned. "Look to my horse," he ordered, as the agitated landlord appeared in answer to the uproar; "and, wait a minute—we shall want another pullet or three. *Pardieu!* By this, my stomach must believe my throat to have been cut."

He dropped down on the bench across from his friend and voraciously attacked the bird that stood between them. With a great mouthful of the fowl noisily masticating, he poured himself a generous stoup of wine and tossed it after the meat. "Eat, Cyrano!" he cried, with a gesture. "Or do we at once resume our quarrel?"

"Nay," laughed the man with the Nose, "there is time enough for that. I would have nothing of a final nature settled for either of us before we had dined. Fall to, and I shall join you without delay."

"Damme, but it is good to see you again," exclaimed D'Artagnan, between mouthfuls. "It seems a full six years, rather than six months, since we have met."

"All of that," agreed his friend. "And I am glad to see *you* again, old comrade. I hope the world has gone well with you?"

"Well enough," shrugged the musketeer. "I am no nearer wealth than ever I was, if that is what you mean; and God knows I am no younger." He leaned across the table. "Do not speak it above a whisper, Cyrano; but in your absence I passed my fortieth year! Do I not have the appearance of one grown suddenly old?"

His companion looked critically at the stalwart frame and the lean features, then laughed heartily.

"Yes, yes," he said, "you are become quite ancient and decrepit, D'Artagnan. Truly, a pathetic sight! And I—gaze sorrowfully, my friend, upon one who is five years your senior. Does it not occur to you that I am slowly fading?"

"Like a rose in drought," cried the musketeer, with a grin. "Poor tottering oldster! Why, I warrant it is all of eight hours since you outrapiered and slew a man!"

"'Tis six," answered De Bergerac thoughtfully. "But, before him, I swear there had been none for a fortnight." He plucked a lace handkerchief from his sleeve and daintily dusted his lips.

D'Artagnan drew his sleeve across his mouth. "And how went the mission overseas, dear boy?"

"Quite admirably. There was difficulty from the beginning to the end. I vow I did nothing but produce bad verses and lose money to the Spaniards at their tables. My game is becoming rotten. Yet His Majesty was good enough to be pleased and to call the mission a success."

"*Parbleu!* I am glad. And now, at length, the six months of our agreed probation is up."

"To-night," agreed De Bergerac, with a smile of pleasure. "It could hardly be better, by the by, since it is privacy above all things that we desire. This storm was heaven-sent to aid us."

"True! I like not the whole of Paris for an audience. It gives one a bad name. Heaven knows, mine is bad enough already. To work, then, old friend, and let this evening's labour determine for all time our difference. *À outrance*, I believe?"

"Quite so! The honour of my company is at stake."

"And mine. The musketeers have placed their faith in me."

They embraced heartily.

"It grieves me to have to slay so old a friend," said De Bergerac, with emotion. "And yet, you did wrong to hold me up to scorn."

"My heart is sad, Cyrano," cried the musketeer. "How I shall miss you! Is there not someone to whom you would wish a note delivered—afterward?"

They dragged the tables away, with heavy noises, and drew their blades from their sheaths. They faced each other in the cleared space under the light. Their long swords crossed. For an instant, the two finest swordsmen of fiction looked deeply into each other's eyes. Then, with terrible agility, the musketeer was in and out under the other's guard. But De Bergerac had fallen back a step, and the thrust was vain. His return stroke was like a flicker of flame, but it met D'Artagnan's guard and was turned aside. And then the exchange of thrust and parry was such as to fill the long chamber with a sonorous clangour, and the thudding of swift feet advancing and retreating was like the sound of a dreadful dance.

A shriek echoed from the kitchen, and the wild-eyed domestic fled wailing to the upper quarters. The landlord, entering the room as his maid quitted it, stood for a time aghast. "Gentlemen! Gentlemen!" he implored, and wrung his hands helplessly. "Holy Virgin!" he moaned. "What can they be quarrelling about? Can it have been the wine?"

But the end was already at hand. Over the high melody of the swords and the pounding of feet, over the roar of the tempest without, sounded suddenly a new voice, the voice of a woman screaming in a chamber above. At the first cry, the landlord turned pale and ran wildly from the room.

"Help, help!" screamed the clear, blonde voice. "I am here—a prisoner! Brave gentlemen, come! I am here. Help, help!"

Upon the instant, the swords of the combatants fell apart. The eyes of the duellists met; they stood staring, their points against the ground.

"Did you hear?" whispered D'Artagnan. "That was no wench, Cyrano, but a lady in desperate trouble."

"She called for our assistance," said De Bergerac hoarsely. "A prisoner—upstairs."

"And the landlord has gone to her!" cried the musketeer. "It is foul play, Cyrano." With a roar, he plunged for the stairway and ran upward, his naked blade still gleaming in his hand. At his heels ran Cyrano de Bergerac, calling reassuringly to the prisoner.

In the dark hallway above, the foremost runner fell over the figure of the landlord, crouched low against the stairhead; but before the knife upraised above the musketeer could fall, De Bergerac had seized the hand that held it. There was a sharp snap, as of a breaking bone, and then a cry as the figure of the host was raised above the head and nose of Cyrano de Bergerac and pitched headlong down the stair pit. The rescuers plunged on.

The screaming had recommenced, and following it to its source, they came upon the locked door to a bedchamber. Then the door fell inward at a touch of D'Artagnan's shoulder, and they stood in the aperture, awaiting they knew not what.

"We are friends, Mademoiselle," said De Bergerac softly, after an instant of silence. "Be assured of that, whoever you may be."

"We have heard your cries and we are come to

rescue you," added D'Artagnan, elbowing his friend aside.

In the darkness, they heard the sound of muffled sobbing, and after a moment a voice, low and thankful. "I am bound," said the voice. "I cannot move. Oh, if you are friends, take me away from here!"

"Stand guard, D'Artagnan, while I fetch a light," said De Bergerac; and presently his feet were heard descending the crooked stairway. In a few minutes, he returned with a lamp, his grotesque shadow with its ludicrous nose preceding him up the flight.

By the light of the lamp, they were enabled to look around the chamber, and in a corner, on a rough bed, they saw the slight figure of a young woman. Her wrists and ankles were firmly tied, and over the folds of a big towel that once had been about her mouth her tousled head thrust upward, set with a pair of frightened, lovely eyes. Upon the instant, D'Artagnan recognized her.

"Mademoiselle de la Motte d'Argencour!" he cried, in amazement.

"Monsieur D'Artagnan!" she exclaimed. "God is good to me. What miracle brings you here to-night? Has the King had word of my abduction?"

"Nay, dear lady," said the musketeer, "or, if so, I have not heard of it. Our rescue was as unpremeditated as it was fortuitous."

"Present me, D'Artagnan," muttered De Bergerac, tugging at his companion's sleeve.

"Ah, of course! Your pardon, *mon ami*, and yours, Mademoiselle. It is my happiness to present the Chevalier Cyrano Savinien Hercule de Bergerac, the uncrowned laureate of our forces."

De Bergerac bowed to the boards. "Would it not be well to release Mademoiselle from her bonds?" he asked. "Permit me!" He stooped and cut the knots with his sword.

"But, dear lady," cried D'Artagnan, "what accident has brought you to this pass? Did you say 'twas an abduction?"

The fair young creature accepted his arm and walked painfully about the chamber, while the blood flowed back into her limbs.

"Abduction, yes," she replied, "and by the Cardinal's orders. The fool believes the King's interest in me is too personal. I tell you this, of course, in confidence."

"Assuredly! Then, Mademoiselle, it shall be our pleasure to return you to your lodging, wherever it may be; later, to call upon the King."

"It was from my lodging I was abducted, and

by the treachery of my guardian. Monsieur D'Artagnan, you must go at once to the King and tell him of my plight."

The musketeer tugged thoughtfully at his small beard. "We cannot leave you here, dear lady," he demurred.

"Mademoiselle is welcome to *my* apartment," cried De Bergerac. "Whatever her plight, she is more than welcome. There is an excellent housekeeper, and some trusted servants. I shall remain the night with *you*, D'Artagnan."

"That is well; but there will be difficulty about seeing His Majesty at this hour. Have you not some small token, Mademoiselle, by which I might be admitted to the presence? Truth to tell, I am at present a little out of favour."

"My ring!" exclaimed Mademoiselle de la Motte d'Argencour. "It was stolen from me when I was spirited away. It was His Majesty's gift."

"Stolen?"

"By the villain who conspired to have me abducted—my guardian, the Vicomte d'Emonville."

D'Artagnan whistled in surprise. "So 'tis d'Emonville we have to thank for this adventure! As it happens, there is an old score between us. Upon my soul, Mademoiselle, I think that we must thank each other for this night." He turned to his companion. "It is my intention, Cyrano, to recover this lady's ring."

"And mine," bowed the Chevalier de Bergerac.

"Good! To horse, then, quickly, and let us first place our young friend in a place of safety. Already we have loitered here too long. We shall be fortunate if we do not have to fight our way to Paris."

"Unfortunate, I should be inclined to suggest, were not Mademoiselle in our protection," amended De Bergerac.

They descended to the lower room, and in an instant there was a further outcry. The landlord had disappeared. In the kitchen, the scullery wench again was rattling her pots.

De Bergerac muttered in his beard. Aloud he said: "The fall alone should have been sufficient to break the scoundrel's neck."

"He has the start of us, none the less," said D'Artagnan. "Quickly, Cyrano, and place the lady on your crupper." He rushed out into the night to capture his horse. In a moment he was back, and smiling.

"After all, it is less serious than I thought," he chuckled. "Our host did indeed attempt to betray us; but he is now beyond such recklessness. He is dead in the stable."

"Dead?"

"He thought to take my horse for his ride to D'Emonville, but the horse thought otherwise. An admirable animal. I won him upon a single cast of the dice. His hoofs are like the crash of artillery."

"Still," observed De Bergerac, "it would be well to get along."

The storm had somewhat abated, but a light rain still fell monotonously. Through its fog they proceeded at a rapid trot toward Paris, and in good time disposed their charge as arranged. Thereafter, they rode briskly toward the dwelling of the Vicomte d'Emonville, who would assuredly have left it had he dreamed what visitors were coming.

"This D'Emonville, Cyrano, is a thorough villain," explained the musketeer. "I have perhaps had more dealings with him than have you. Believe me, it will give me happiness to slay him, should he refuse our request for Mademoiselle's ring."

"He is an erudite scoundrel, I have heard," said De Bergerac. "A scholar, and a dabbler in the sciences. Is he also a swordsman?"

"One of the best. Twice our blades have crossed, and I have promised him that the third time shall be the last. He must not expect to live forever."

"His ward is very lovely," sighed the second horseman. "She looked askance, I fear, at my poor nose."

"Tut!" said the musketeer. "She is the King's. And yet, I grant you, she is a delicious morsel. I *felt* my age, Cyrano, what time I gazed at her."

"And I, until *she* looked at *me*," said his companion. " 'Tis amazing how a woman's glance can set the pulse to fluttering. When I touched her hand, I thought I was a boy again."

"Ay," nodded D'Artagnan, "we are a queer lot. Even our mirrors lie to us. I glance in mine, to knot a scarf, or cut the little hairs in my nostrils, and lo! instead of D'Artagnan, the aging captain, I see that firebrand youth of Gascony, who came to Paris twenty years ago. So insensible has been the change that I am still that hawk-faced boy, and only when I am severely jolted do I realize the gulfs that lie between us. Last evening, I courted a young widow for an hour, thinking how well I understood the task, and how successfully my suit was making out; only to find her slightly flattered and amused. 'You are a nice old man,' she told me. 'I really like you very much indeed.' She keeps her favours for some scoundrelly lieutenant."

Riding more slowly as they approached their destination, the two friends dismounted at length before the handsome edifice, and stood for a moment looking upward.

"The household has retired," said Cyrano in a low voice. "We must knock them up, D'Artagnan."

He turned to find that his companion had vanished around a corner of the street. In a moment the musketeer was back. "Pst! Cyrano!" he whispered. "There is a little light, low down, on t'other side. Someone keeps late hours, in a queer corner, 'twould seem."

They trod softly to the spot. The light, when they looked upon it, was a thin slit shining from an embrasure well shuttered against the public, and so low that the room from which it emanated appeared below the level of the street. A door gave on to the pavement near at hand, but it was stoutly barred and bolted.

Above, a balcony of twisted metal projected; beyond it a pair of tall windows rose upward, ghostly in the rain. With a spring, D'Artagnan seized the metalwork at its lowest point and writhed swiftly over the rail; then, bending, assisted his heavier companion to follow. The windows creaked faintly and yielded to their touch. With infinite patience, the musketeer picked with his knife at the catch between the panels, and in a little time saw them swing gently away from him. Stepping softly, the intruders gained the room beyond, and quietly reclosed the windows.

Intense blackness confronted them. It stretched away from them on every side. It rolled forward and receded in waves and billows. There was no saying what lay an inch in either direction. But when their eyes had become accustomed to the gloom, they pushed slowly forward in the direction of the stairway that they knew must lead downward to the secret chamber. Brushing past chair and table, they came at length upon a doorway that gave upon a corridor, and passing through, found themselves at the head of a small flight that curved downward into darkness.

"Cautiously, *mon ami*," whispered the musketeer, his lips against the other's ear. "We are not certain that it is the master, himself, who burns so late a lamp." Then, shadowlike, they began to descend the stair.

When two turns had been made in darkness, the light again revealed itself. This time it was an upright slot, about the height of a tall man. The door that led into the secret chamber stood ajar. Listening closely, they heard within small sounds that told of occupancy. Then, stepping forward in the coolness of the lower level, D'Artagnan placed an eye against the aperture and looked inside. It was his good fortune to find the room's inhabitant within view.

Attired in a sable robe, sprinkled with yellow stars and crescent moons, the Vicomte d'Emonville sat at a table covered with a heavy cloth, his eyes bent in complete absorption upon a parchment strip that lay before him. A gleaming vial of no great size, but richly jewelled, stood at his elbow; the light by which he read was a flare of flame that leaped upward from a cruet of oil suspended from above. A shelf of books was near at hand, and, glancing upward, D'Artagnan saw without surprise the suspended skin of an alligator, stuffed, hideous, and lifelike. Against the wall was fastened the heavy shell of a tortoise, the body of a bat, a stuffed owl, and other strange creatures that he had heard about but never seen. All were dead; the chamber itself seemed damp and dead. Save for the motionless figure of the man at the table, the only visible life was that evidenced by a yellow cat that sat at the scholar's feet and purred harshly. There could be no mistaking the import of the sight upon which the musketeer gazed: the place was the secret study of an alchemist and astrologer. The Vicomte d'Emonville was in league with the Devil.

With a gentle pressure of the arm, to insure caution, D'Artagnan gave place to his companion, and De Bergerac in turn stared into the strange museum. The scholar had stirred; now he was looking earnestly at the glittering vial, which he held within his hands. His eyes gleamed with a feverish light. Obviously, this was some new and curious thing that was engaging his midnight attention. De Bergerac's amazement grew.

D'Artagnan, returning to the peephole, hesitated for thirty seconds; then swung the door open to its widest sweep and stepped into the chamber, drawing his sword as he entered.

"Give you good-evening, Monsieur le Vicomte," said he pleasantly. "May one inquire what fascinating subject engages your so-diligent attention? Is it a love philtre that you have discovered in a tomb, or a new poison for the King's birthday?"

With a strange cry, the astrologer sprang upright and faced his most implacable enemy. In the shadows behind his friend, De Bergerac stood, smiling an evil smile. The flickering yellow beams that illumined his surprising nose, gave it the hue of ancient ivory. The yellow cat, frightened by the intrusion, had bounded into a dark corner, from which its eyes now gleamed maliciously. Recovering his self-possession, the master of the mansion sardonically bowed.

"If I am not mistaken," said he politely, "it is the celebrated Captain D'Artagnan, himself. And your companion, Captain, although unknown to me, I should guess by his nose to be the no less celebrated Chevalier de Bergerac. You will correct me if I am wrong. The light, however, falls sharply upon your blades, gentlemen; it dazzles my eyes. Since there are two of you, and I am myself un-armed, will you not return them to their scab-bards?"

"*Touché!*" smiled the musketeer and slapped home his sword, an example which his companion followed. "But we have not come, Monsieur le Vicomte, for an exchange of deadly compliments. It is merely to request a certain ring that we have ventured to intrude upon your privacy."

"A ring? You surprise me."

"Quite so! The ring of Mademoiselle de la Motte d'Argencour, your ward. You need feel no hesitancy in yielding it, since we are come with the request from the lady herself."

"But that is impossible," cried the Vicomte d'Emonville. "Mademoiselle is, I trust, upstairs at this moment, asleep."

"She is at this moment asleep, I also trust,"

said D'Artagnan, "but she is not upstairs. No, my dear D'Emonville, there is no time for parley and discussion. We know what we know, and the ring we are determined to have. You removed it from the lady's hand, not many hours ago; to be exact, shortly before you caused her to be removed to a most disreputable inn, conducted by one Gaston Dubois, not far from Jammes."

The Vicomte gestured angrily. "If Dubois has told you any such outrageous tale," he began, "he shall be——"

"Slain? We have spared you that effort. Dubois is already dead and damned. But it was not Dubois who informed us. I have told you that it was Mademoiselle de la Motte d'Argencour, herself."

"The King's plaything!" sneered the Vicomte suddenly.

"Not so fast, Monsieur le Vicomte," said D'Artagnan, restraining himself with an effort. "We are all playthings of the King, it is well to remember, and our heads are at his disposal. With the political aspects of the matter, however, we have no concern. It is the ring that we are patiently requesting."

"And if I refuse to yield it?"

D'Artagnan shrugged. "I shall not conceal from you my earnest wish that you will so refuse," he replied, "since in that case, I shall have pleasure in slitting your throat and taking it anyway."

"And if I give it up?"

"We shall have no choice, I fear, but to go away, although I warn you that your fate would only be postponed."

"What a cutthroat you have become, D'Artagnan!" cried the astrologer. He threw off his long, encumbering robe and faced them in his shirt-sleeves.

Arguing blandly, the Vicomte d'Emonville retreated to the far wall, upon which within easy reach hung his polished sword. Now, quickly, he sprang forward, snatched it from its place, and, whirling, launched himself with incredible speed upon the musketeer. But D'Artagnan was awaiting him. Before the menace of the musketeer's blade, D'Emonville fell back and lowered his point. His small eyes turned cunningly from one to the other of his enemies.

"Since either way I am disgraced, gentlemen," he said, at length, "I am left but little choice. Is it your intention to murder me?"

"It is our intention to recover Mademoiselle's ring," answered D'Artagnan patiently. "You are beginning to take a philosophical view of the matter, however, and so I offer you a chance for life. The ring we must have, in any case; but if you can kill me, your life shall be your own. The Chevalier de Bergerac will then receive the ring from your hands and you shall be allowed to escape the country, if you can."

"Nay," cried De Bergerac, in dismay, "am I to have no hand in the blood-letting?"

"Only if, after slaying me, our friend refuses still to yield the ring. In which unlikely case, I should have no hesitation about running him through, were he defenseless and unarmed."

For a time, the Vicomte stood gnawing at his moustache. "Very well," he said, at last, "let it be so. The ring is here, upon my little finger. Take it from me who can!" And falling quickly into position, he made a thrust at the musketeer that almost took him off his guard.

But hardly had the blades engaged when the astrologer's weapon was twisted from his hand and flung crashing against the masonry of the wall. His adversary bowed.

"A trick of the wrist," said D'Artagnan, "which I am sure you would not permit again. Pick up your sword."

Again the blades crossed, and the devil's game went on. De Bergerac, in the doorway, had set his back against the boards to guard against intrusion.

With expert eye, he watched the dazzling exchange of thrust and parry. The clangour of the steel filled the chamber and echoed back from its walls; the patter of the dancing feet was continuous and deadly; the breathing of the combatants became an eerie pattern of sound. Still each remained upright and intact, and so equally were the duellists matched that the single watcher could scarcely restrain a cheer when one or the other performed some miracle of recovery.

"If I should live to be a thousand," murmured De Bergerac, with appreciation, "I should never again see such a fight!"

But when forty minutes had passed away without an advantage, the end came suddenly and more swiftly than the eye could follow. D'Emonville himself did not know what had happened until he felt his opponent's blade stand out a foot beyond and between his shoulders. Then the sword was deftly withdrawn, and the scholar-noble gasped once and pitched forward upon his face.

"*Finis!*" said D'Artagnan, panting; and, stooping, he took the King's ring from the hand of the astrologer.

No sound disturbed the stillness of the house above them. The floors were stout and thick, the walls impregnable. It was an admirable tomb that the Vicomte d'Emonville had builded for himself.

For an instant, the adventurers stood listening, then D'Artagnan turned to the door. "Let us go," he said.

"A moment," cried De Bergerac. "I am curious to know what mysteries engaged our philosophic knave." He strode to the table and looked down upon the parchment sheet that the dead man had studied. As he read, his face became a mask of astonishment. Muttering incredulously, he seated himself before the table.

"What is it, *mon ami?*" asked the musketeer curiously. "Have you discovered the secret of transmuting the baser metals?" He leaned across the other's shoulder and let his eyes run across the script. "It is Latin," he cried, in disgust. "I cannot read it."

De Bergerac turned upward a pair of eyes that shone with startled triumph. "Listen," he said in a whisper. "I will read it to you!

"I, Dominic Oviedo, of the Order of Saint Dominic, bequeath this vial to him who shall have the courage to employ it. It is of the Devil, I make no doubt; yet it was given me as the veritable waters of the fabled fountain of Bimini . . ."

He continued to the end, his voice rising as he progressed, then sank back in his chair, his eyes upon his companion. D'Artagnan was breathing heavily.

"*Pardieu!*" cried the musketeer, at length. "It is madness, Cyrano! It is beyond belief." He snatched the vial from the table and devoured it with his eyes. On a slender band of gold, he read in his own language the significant words, neatly inscribed by some sharp-pointed instrument. . . . *L'Eau de Bimini.*

"There are many things that are beyond belief, my friend," said Cyrano de Bergerac. "Yet our scholars search them out and read their secrets. They are beyond belief only until we have proved them credible. For my part, I think we have arrested our late adversary at perhaps the pinnacle of his career."

"But how came *he* by this vial and this paper?"

"God knows!" shrugged Cyrano, studying the vial in his turn. "No doubt there are other strange things about this creepy chamber, had we the wit and time to hunt them out. Yet, I am satisfied with this single discovery. Bethink you, D'Artagnan," he cried almost fiercely. "Not long ago, we jested of our age, and while it is not great, we are no longer chickens. Now we hold within our hands the secret of the ages! From the dawn of time, this miracle has been sought by man. The secret of eternal youth! It makes a mock of Death and Dissolution. It laughs at Time. With the priests we can cry, 'O Death where is thy sting, O Grave where is thy victory!'"

"*Diable !*" cried D'Artagnan, catching the contagion. "We are more powerful than the Pope himself."

His companion stroked the huge promontory that dominated his face. For a time, he was silent; then he rose briskly to his feet.

"It is yours," he said, "and mine. Our quarrel is at an end. There is no difference between us. Immortal, we shall watch the centuries unfold. Let us begone before in some fashion this miracle is undone."

They donned their cloaks and went out into the night. Mounting their waiting animals, they clattered away through the silent, narrow streets. No words were exchanged between them. Only the rattle of their horses' hoofs woke the echoes in old walls and buildings. The rain had ceased to fall. The moon now rode high over Paris, tricking out its fantastic roofs and spires in silver light. It glinted on the dark stream flowing sullenly beneath its bridges. The minds of the horsemen raced with the swiftly moving silver clouds.

The musketeer drew a long breath and broke the silence. "Cyrano," said he, "what are your plans, if this amazing draught prove potent?"

"An it restore to me a beauty that was never mine," sighed De Bergerac, "to lay my heart at the feet of the fairest maid in France, and offer her an eternity of devotion. And yours?"

D'Artagnan laughed happily. "To lay my heart at the feet of every maid in Christendom, and offer her the same."

His companion shuddered. "What a passion you have for trouble," he exclaimed.

In time they came upon a scene of merriment, and it was their misfortune to be thirsty. With the waters of the fountain of Bimini in their possession, they bent their heads under the lintel of a small hostelry and demanded wine. From all corners flocked the friendly musketeers to toast their hero.

"D'Artagnan!" they cheered.

"We must hasten," said D'Artagnan. "One round, brave lads, and then we must be going."

"But where have you been, old rooster?" asked one Porthos, in a booming bass. "We looked for you, high and low, some hours ago."

"King's business, or the business of a lady?" drawled the affected tenor of one who went by the name of Aramis.

"Or, perhaps, both!" smiled one called Athos, clapping an arm about the shoulders of his friend.

"Faith, it is somewhat as you suspect, comrades," answered D'Artagnan, "and yet the strangest matter which has befallen concerns neither King nor lady. It is the maddest thing that ever yet has occurred to man. What say you, Cyrano? Shall we tell them?"

"Why not? They are your friends and mine. Let them rejoice with us."

"Then, hear ye, Musketeers! 'Tis the oddest adventure that you can very well imagine. What would you give, my hearties, for a draught of water, crystal pure?"

"A fig!" cried Porthos, with a thundering laugh.

"Nay, but if it were potent to render you forever beautiful and young!"

"Good wine is better," murmured Aramis, and verified his preference from a flagon at hand.

"Tush!" said D'Artagnan. "'Tis no matter for jesting." And sitting astraddle upon a bench, he related the high history of the vial, being careful only to omit the exact nature of the transaction by which it had come into their possession.

A roar of laughter greeted his recital. "Oh, admirable! Exquisite! Tell us another, D'Artagnan," cheered the musketeers.

"By the mass, 'tis true, none the less," cried their captain indignantly. "Show them the very trinket, Cyrano."

The vial was passed from hand to hand with many exclamations of admiration for its beauty.

"And now the parchment!"

In solemn tones the words of Dominic Oviedo were chanted to the audience of drunkards.

The neglected vial, meanwhile, sat where it had been placed, upon a corner of the table and not far from an open window. As the reader finished his translation, there arose outside the shop a sudden commotion and angry voices calling.

"A fight!" roared the company, in ecstasy, and rushed headlong from the inn, leaving the story-tellers staring at the doorway through which they had vanished.

It was in this moment, while all backs were turned, that a lean brown arm, bare to the elbow, was plunged through the open window. Thin fingers closed upon the vial's throat and lifted it swiftly into the night. Its captors, turning an instant later, looked blankly at the spot where it had stood.

"The vial!" cried De Bergerac. "D'Artagnan, it is gone!"

The musketeer stared stupidly. "*Mon Dieu!*" he muttered. "'Tis magic! I vow 'twas there only a moment since."

"And now 'tis gone," added De Bergerac hoarsely. "Am I mad, D'Artagnan? Did we ever have it?"

Each looked into the other's face with a wild surmise. Had the wine indeed been so potent? Had there ever been an inn and an interrupted duel, a lady and a rescue, a dead alchemist and a jewelled vial? Were they, themselves, perhaps, only the latest chapter in a fantastic novel?

"What now, Cyrano?" cried D'Artagnan. "What now is left to us?"

"There is the ring," said the Chevalier de Bergerac; "and there is the parchment." He brought the latter up from his pocket. "May the devil take them both!"

CHAPTER EIGHT

IN WHICH A POET MAKES LOVE AND A HIGH-WAYMAN MAKES TROUBLE

"I don't know how great you may be," said the Guinea man, "but I don't like your looks: I have often bought a man much better than you, all muscles and bones, for ten guineas."
—THE REV. WILLIAM WARBURTON.

And now the high history of the vial must cross the channel, and skipping as many years as make up the appointed lifetime of a man, resume its career under new skies and in the company of new figures. And first we have to do with a whimsical episode in the life of a gentleman of letters, which somehow has escaped the more sober commentators, or has been relegated to a footnote as open to some question.

Among the several chariots that upon one errand or another rolled out of London on an evening while yet the second George reigned quietly at Hampton Court, there was one that headed eastward along the river road as if for that residence of royalty, itself. It was, however, destined only

175

for Twickenham, a sprawling village celebrated
for nothing more remarkable than that it tolerated
two of the most distinguished and eccentric poets
of the age. Indeed, as it proceeded, at economic
speed and without ostentation, toward its mark,
it actually jounced within its bowels those celebrated poets, who were, as it happened, of opposite
sexes.

As the lights of the city dwindled in the distance
and became sparks on the horizon, the conversation languished and was succeeded by the heavy
import of silence. Each felt that epigrams im-
pended and was dismayed.

The road paralleled the windings of the river,
which flowed peacefully upon the right. On the left,
the heavy timber of the forest glanced past and
fell behind, mile after mile. The hoofs of the bay
geldings thudded monotonously in the king's highway, and the sounds of passage died without echo.

Milady, midnight-browed and fiercely handsome, reclined against the cushions in a corner.
Her bright, quizzical eyes rested with queer regard
on the pale face of her companion, a grotesquely
twisted little man who sat upright like a child
upon a pillow. The man's legs did not reach to
the floor of the carriage, and when the wheels
triumphed over besetting stones and hillocks, he

bounced like india rubber in his seat. His brilliant eyes gleamed in the moonlight. For a moment he closed them and lay back against the cushions.

"You spoke," his high, thin voice ascended, "of a new poem upon which you planned to break a quill."

The handsome features of the lady cleared.

"A curious matter," she answered. "When I was in Constantinople, with my husband, I saw there a bit of parchment, which set forth a most romantic tale. It was the history of a small vial, lost these hundred years, and the water that it contained was said to be that of a fabled fountain in the isle of Bimini, by whose virtues youth and vigour were restored to such as drank of it. But the vial was missing, and none knew where to find it. Hence, perhaps, the fact that I grow no younger."

"The quack Thomson should hear of it," cried her companion. "He has all but ruined me with his physicks and his pills. But, indeed, you grow younger as you grow older, Lady Mary! How came the document to Constantinople, I wonder? The legend, as I remember it, was Spanish."

"Its history was known to the French gentleman who owned it. It once belonged to a Parisian bravo, a notorious fellow, who, it seems, had it from an alchemist. The bravo, one De Bergerac, from whom the vial was stolen almost as he was planning to drink of it, had no further interest in the parchment, and so handed it, in time, to his only surviving friend, a musketeer called Aramis, who later became an abbé. The abbé, in turn, handed on the document to his son, who in his own turn gave it to my friend, a collector of autographs."

"And the vial?"

"Was stolen, as I have said, from De Bergerac, who no doubt had stolen it himself. So runs the pretty tale! Where it is now, be sure that I have no idea, else it should grace my boudoir. Two drops a day, in private, after breakfast, would be about right. But you see its possibilities as a romantic poem."

"I could do with a drop or two, myself," confessed the other poet wryly. "It is, as you suggest, however, no bad notion for a poem. I shall think about it. Perhaps we could do it together, eh?"

He closed his eyes again, and for a time was silent. Then a spasm of savage mirth contorted the long face, and he reopened the dialogue.

"A lively little creature, with long legs and arms; a spider would be no ill emblem of him. He has been taken at a distance for a small windmill!"

Lady Montagu was startled. "What do you mean?" she asked, and thrust her own head from the other window. "What is it you suggest?"

But the placid ribbon of the Thames, with its wooded isles, and the peaceful road that flowed beside it, were all that met her gaze. On Mr. Pope's side, the forest still stretched away, unbroken.

" 'Twas here that Bolingbroke suffered his mishap," continued the poet. "His coach broke down, and while it was undergoing repairs, a highwayman stepped from the wood and relieved the philosopher of that which, in his verses, he had so long despised: to wit, his wealth. There was some small dispute, and His Lordship's body servant received a ball through the shoulder."

"Good heavens!" said the Lady Mary. "I remember there was some talk of it. Is the fellow so dangerous?"

"A veritable demon, I am given to understand. Particularly with the ladies, to whom he pays court with a rough gallantry that some have found not unpleasant. I thought 'twere as well to be prepared."

"Pope, tell me the truth: is that weapon loaded?"

"To the brim, with slugs. It will blow him into powder."

"It will destroy the carriage and us all!" cried the lady. "What knowledge have you of such matters, Pope? Hand it at once to the driver!"

"Nay," said the poet, "let me have my hour, and you shall see how a child, a cripple, a mountebank can behave. It may be that he will not appear."

"Before God, I believe you are raving mad," said the Lady Mary. "If he appears———"

The carriage stopped with a suddenness that bit off the words between her teeth and flung them both forward into the pit. The procession of trees upon the left had stopped, and now stood starkly in the moonlight, as if marking time. Over the dancing hoof beats of a horse, a brutal voice was raised in altercation with the driver. Then a masked face appeared at the poet's window: a man was leaning over from a horse's back, and the great mouth of a blunderbuss was looking in at them.

"A pretty pair, by my faith!" roared the highwayman jovially. "A pretty face and a purse of golden guineas. Step down, if you please, sweet birdlings, and let me have a better look at you."

Milady Montagu sank swooning into her corner. As in a nightmare, she heard the voice of Mr. Pope replying. With horror, she saw the frail hand of Mr. Pope thrust the hideous weapon aside.

"You animal!" shrilled the high-pitched voice of the poet. "You impudent villain! You insufferable scoundrel! You curd of ass's milk! You ape, dog, monkey, pig, wolf, and abortion! Get gone before I fill you with enough slugs to nail you to the earth!"

Saying which, he brought up his own weapon with incredible rapidity, and discharged it so close to the marauder's ear that the man started away in terror. The hail of slugs poured into the forest with a noise like a sudden shower, clipping the leaves and branches so that they fell crackling to the ground. The highwayman's horse reared and plunged, carrying its rider across the road at a single bound, then under the urge of sudden spurs darted off in a turning of the wood and disappeared.

"And, I should have added, *coward !*" continued Mr. Pope, quietly dusting his cuffs. He put his head out of the window. "Drive on, Thomas; and if there are any further disturbances, pull up and leave the situation to your master."

For a time, thereafter, they drove forward in silence. Out of a corner of his eye, the poet watched

his companion's face and purred contentedly. The
lady's emotions were open to the world. Mingled
with her astonishment, there was a definite admiration. Pope's eyes rested complacently on the
white hand that had been withdrawn from his own.
In spite of her admiration for his genius, he reflected, this magnificent creature had never taken
his suit quite seriously. He had been a child whose
head she had metaphorically patted whenever his
emotion had threatened to overflow. "There,
there!" she had said, in effect. "There, there!"
Sometimes she had said it aloud. Now it was
different. He could read in her eyes the reproach
with which she was filled, for her conduct. She was
self-conscious and ashamed. It would be difficult
for her to say what she felt, but he would make it
easy for her. The tremble of her lower lip was delicious; the droop of her lashes maddening. They
were quite alone.

There was her infernal husband, of course; but,
after all, they were living apart. If report could
be believed, the lady would scarcely be offended
by any suggestion of disloyalty. How admirably
Peterborough had arranged matters! But the man
had a genius for such things. Good old Peterborough! What a villain he was with the ladies, to
be sure!

A thought of the long-lost vial of youth drifted across the poet's mind, and he smiled a little cynically at the interest the subject had evoked from his companion. Youth rioted in his own veins. He felt ten years younger than he had ever been in his life.

Tentatively, he stretched forth a hand in the darkness.

The carriage stopped again, this time more soberly. It had proceeded no more than a mile.

"Pope!" shrieked the Lady Mary frantically, pushing her head out of the window and instantly withdrawing it. "Your pistol—quick!"

A second horror appeared suddenly at the poet's window, and a voice charged with a sinister significance demanded the poet's purse. Mr. Pope gasped and cried out between alarm and indignation.

"You fool! You ass!" he hissed. "What do you mean by this? Was not once enough?"

A long arm reached in through the aperture and seized the poet by the lace at his throat, dragging him close to the window. The devilish masked face of the second bandit bent close to the pale face of Mr. Pope, which became even whiter.

"*Mean*, little toad?" sneered the heavy voice above him. "Why, marry, that I have stopped you on the king's highway, little toad, and shall presently slit your throat with my little finger nail."

The teeth of Mr. Pope rattled in his head. "It was not ordered," he stammered, half strangled by the clutch upon his throat. "I tell you it was not to be! Only once was ordered, good sir! I swear to you that was the agreement."

"Before God," swore the highwayman, "if you do not at once cease your bleating and yield me up your purse, I shall twist your neck as if it were a pullet's!"

"It was a jest!" clamoured the poet wildly. "For God's sake, listen to me and I will explain."

The iron hand twisted the lace at his throat and strangled further outcry.

"Let him go, Mr. Highwayman," said a clear voice from the depths of the carriage. "What money we have is here with me. I give it to you gladly. This—this gentleman—is a poet and, as you observe, a cripple. He has nothing to give you, be assured. Will you accept my word?"

The horseman released his prisoner and, straightening in his saddle, swept off his plumed hat. He bowed to the neck of his animal and, dismounting, leered in at the window.

"Before God, miss," he vowed, "I did not see your face! I supposed you to be the boy's grandmother. Slit me, now, but this is generous of you! I am almost tempted to return it to you. But doubtless you can afford it. I am a poor man, reduced by circumstances to this night-riding. As loyal a subject as the King—God bless him!—can boast. Is there, perhaps, some little trinket of your own that you might spare me as a souvenir? A pin, a ring, perhaps—— Ah, thanks! The money will soon go, but this I shall always wear upon my finger in memory of your kindness to an unfortunate man, down on his luck. Look after the little fellow, miss. I think he is a trifle off his head."

He bowed gallantly and, swinging into his saddle, once more doffed his beaver and rode away in the moonlight.

Milady Montagu put her head out of the window for the third time. "Drive on, Thomas," she said drily, "and if there are any further disturbances, don't stop if you can get through."

"Yes, Milady," answered Thomas.

"Drive to Twickenham."

"Yes, Milady," answered Thomas again.

"Drive like hell!"

"Yes, Milady," answered Thomas for the third time.

She sank back in her seat as the horses were

lashed into a gallop, and for a little time was silent. Then a low laugh bubbled in her throat and issued from her lips like the song of a bird. She put her hands to her face and screamed with laughter.

"Oh, Pope, Pope!" she cried between paroxysms. "You will be the death of me yet. Two of them! One after the other! Like bill collectors! And the second one so unexpected! Only one had been ordered! Oh, dear, oh, dear!"

After a moment, when there had come no response from the poet's corner, she asked: "With whom was the arrangement made?"

"I have nothing to say to you, Madame," said the poet. He was shaking with the torment of wounded vanity, and could find no recourse save in a fatuous dignity.

"A pity," sighed the Lady Mary, "for indeed there is much that with profit might be said. You might, for instance, tell me that the first performance was calculated to enlist my admiration for your valour, the second my pity for your weakness. Your wits, Alexander, are ordinarily more agile."

But Mr. Pope made no reply, and in a little while she heard him sobbing quietly to himself. The sound at first infuriated her, so that she longed to strike him; then her heart melted, and she could have joined him at his weeping. Between the two emotions a laugh struggled. It was all so absurd! After a time she stretched a hand to him and gently touched the maimed shoulder.

"There, there!" she said; and after another moment, "There, there!"

But there was no answer until, in the moonlight, the straggling outskirts of Twickenham appeared beyond the carriage windows. Then, suddenly, he seized her hand again and dewed it with his kisses. There was a passion on his lips that knotted her brows.

"Have done with foolishness, Pope," she cried sharply. "Has not the evening been sufficiently ridiculous?"

"I love you!" moaned the cripple. "Have you no words of comfort for me?"

Milady Montagu's flesh revolted. The pet ape was going to be troublesome, at last. "Among other things," she replied coldly, "you forget that I have a husband who still lives and flourishes."

"And sins," added the poet, "as do we all. I forget nothing. You despise me because I am ugly and deformed."

"Have it so, then, if you will," she shrugged. "'Tis a pity that you are not tall and beautiful, that your idea might be tested. Perhaps there is something in it. Well, there is the vial with its magic waters. If you have a mind to try a venture, you might go upon the quest. Bring me the vial, Pope, and perhaps I shall be of a different temper." She laughed silverly. "In any case, I bequeath you the poem."

"We are approaching your villa," said the poet stiffly. "I shall walk with you to your door. Believe me, I am sorry if I have caused you any annoyance."

But he was not very sorry. Such sorrow as he felt was for himself, for he knew that, within a week-end, the story would have spread through England. What capital his enemies would make of the incident! There would be a vast buzz in the coffee houses. A malignant hatred filled him as he drove homeward from her dwelling. His wily brain schemed furiously the undoing of the woman who was about to make him ludicrous. No mere lampoon would accomplish his purpose. No subtle and anonymous communication to the press. She must be driven out of England. The very ends of the earth must be made for her untenable.

With grating wheels, the carriage turned inward. Through the trees of his estate, the lights of the villa shone brightly against the darkness. They were on in all parts of the house. Good God! The hour must be close upon midnight. What craziness

was this? Upon this night of all within the year!
Was someone ill?

He fumbled at the catch of the carriage door,
and it swung open as he reached the house. The
house door flew open with a bang, and a little knot
of men struggled through, laughing boisterously.

"Ha, Pope!" cried the foremost, at sight of the
raging poet. "A nice hour for you to be getting
home, this is! We have been waiting for you for
an hour." It was the Earl of Peterborough, his
rollicking friend.

"Where the devil have you been?" continued
the Earl, and he winked knowingly. "His Highness
is within and waits to greet you."

His Highness! It was the long-threatened, long-
impending visit of His Highness. The Prince of
Wales had arrived to talk of poetry with Mr.
Pope.

The poet stepped forward and pressed his lips
against the Earl's ear. "Say nothing of this evening!" he hissed savagely, and stepped away.
Smiling malevolently, Mr. Pope strode into the
presence.

The fat and languid princeling was ensconced
within a chair, surrounded by his bored compan-
ions. He rose and extended a benevolent hand.

"Ha, Pope!" cried the Prince, clapping him

affectionately upon the shoulder. "I'm very glad to see you. Damme, if I'm not! You shall make us laugh, *hein?* We were weary at Richmond, this evening, but the good Williamson had an idea. 'Let us drop in upon our neighbour, Mr. Pope,' he said. Did you not, Williamson? I have been reading a little in your books of poetry, Pope, and I like them well. They are indeed very good. You know, I dabble a bit, myself, in the same stream, ha, ha!"

The poet bowed. "I am delighted to hear Your Highness say so," he drawled insolently. "The fact is, I rather like them myself. I am charmed to find myself in such distinguished company. May I ask what Your Highness has been reading of mine?"

"Your poems, Pope," answered the good Williamson. "What the devil else would His Highness be reading? His Highness reads all that he can find of them. Only the other night, he picked up a volume and called my attention to one that he particularly fancied. A demmed good one, too, filled with nymphs and what-not, you know. An odd volume, a sort of pick-me-up, you know. Ha, ha! A sort of pick-me-up and lay-me-down, you know. Not so bad, that! An annual, I believe, comprising the works of many, and among them one of your own, which His Highness at once singled out for praise."

"I recall it," said the poet. "'The Muse's Bed-chamber,' or some such title. Such volumes serve a useful purpose. They are particularly serviceable to poets, who, like other thieves, escape by getting into a crowd."

"Haw!" roared the good Williamson, in appreciation. "Did I not say, Your Highness, that Mr. Pope would make us laugh? What a fellow you are, Pope!"

The poet sneered and bowed. A shadow lay across the Prince's brow, and he crossed his fat knees nervously. "You have been a writing man all your life, I think, Pope?" he inquired mildly.

"And all Your Highness's. Posterity will remember me, perhaps, as the first professional man of letters, and by Your Highness's midnight visit to do me honour. Yes, I was born to the trade. My mother once told me that. It is an amusing anecdote, and you will enjoy it. It seems that I was born half dead. Indeed, the physician who attended her thought that there was no life within me. And so I was wrapped hastily in a news sheet and thrust out of sight beneath the bed, until some stir betrayed me. It was my first appearance in print."

He bowed again, profoundly, and concluded: "And now, gentlemen, since you have heard my

unimportant history, and I am greatly fatigued,
I shall ask your permission to retire."

The Prince's jaw sagged, and upon the brow
of Williamson, the dancing master, a portentous
frown appeared.

"Now, now, Pope!" cried the latter. "Don't
turn us off like that, you know. His Highness has
taken a great fancy to you and would like to hear
you read some of your poems. There was one
in particular, Your Highness—ah—something
about——?"

"An Indian!" said His Highness, brightening.
Apologetically, he explained: "I have always had
a deep interest in Indians, Mr. Pope. Since I was
a boy, they have fascinated me."

"Come, Pope, let's have the one about the
Indian," chuckled the dancing master. "A demmed
good one, I'm sure."

"You set me an easy task, Your Highness," said
the poet, with a smile. "It is a couplet from my
'Essay on Man,' and very popular with my
admirers:

"Lo, the poor Indian! whose untutored mind
Clothes him in front, and leaves him bare behind!

I thank Your Highness for imposing no greater
strain upon my memory, and I have the honour
to wish you all good-night."

Before anyone could protest, he had bowed himself out of the chamber and disappeared, leaving his admirers to apologize for him as best they could.

In the morning, rising at an unholy hour, Mr. Pope called querulously for a sheaf of paper, and, biting thoughtfully at a new quill, composed himself before his table. For some time he sat thinking, then, twisting his thin legs around the sides of his chair, he dipped his quill into the ink bottle and wrote a single word: *Bimini*.

In this fashion were born the immortal stanzas of that title, since lost, in which the Lady Mary Montagu was celebrated as the noblest creature of her sex since Christ's mother dwelled upon the globe. He put the poem carefully away in his portfolio with instructions for its publication after his death. Leaning back in his chair, he smiled the superior and enlightened smile of one who comprehends the fragile texture of illusions, the venality of women, and the vanity of love.

"Spence," he observed, to the closest of his satellites, who had dropped in for breakfast, "all women are widows at heart. Have nothing to do with them."

It was excellent advice, but it came too late to save poor Spence, who was already married.

"Some day, I shall die, and the world will mourn," continued Mr. Pope. "On that day, you will serve me best by giving to the world a poem that I have written, which is called 'Bimini.' It is about an island that does not exist, and a fountain that never was, by the dubious virtues of whose mythical waters the questionable gift of youth was restored to idiots who feared to die. Principally, it is about a woman who never existed, save only in my twisted brain, but whom—God help me!—I have loved and shall always love."

At this point, to the dismay of Mr. Joseph Spence, he placed his face in the crook of his elbow, upon the table, and burst into tears. Then, retiring to a grotto that he had caused to be builded beneath the London road, where it passed through his estate, he gave himself over to the composition of his astounding "Essay on Woman," which is also lost. The lengthy poem occupied his time at intervals, until within a few days of his death, which occurred some years afterward, and very peacefully.

When that final dispensation was imminent, there were gathered at his bedside most of the poet's friends that remained to him, all of whom wept bitterly and asked him how he felt. To which he replied that he entertained no fears, since there was a reasonable hope of his going to a good place, and an absolute certainty of his leaving a very bad one.

"I am so certain of the soul's being immortal," he said, "that I seem to feel it within me, as it were by intuition."

"Indeed," ventured the physician who was killing him, "I believe you are greatly improved, my dear sir. Your symptoms, for some hours past, have been excellent."

"I am dying of an hundred good symptoms," answered the poet, smiling, and shortly fell into his last delirium.

When he had been dead for ten minutes, there was delivered at the villa, by the post, a small parcel carrying a French postmark, accompanied by a letter in a woman's hand, but unsigned.

" 'Tis a little gift," said Mr. Spence, between his tears. "An admirer, who wishes to remain nameless, begs to send it to Mr. Pope in memory of their early friendship. By a remarkable coincidence, she writes, she encountered it in a Paris pawnshop, where it was supposed to be an ancient vial of perfume."

He opened the packet, and the mourners at the bier of Mr. Pope looked with curiosity upon a golden vial of curious workmanship, set with tiny, flashing gems. Its stopper was sealed with red wax, and the antiquity of the trinket was apparent to them all. On a curving strip of the dull metal, the clergyman, Warburton, deciphered a line of mediæval French, somewhat worn but still faintly legible. He made shift to translate its message as "Waters of Bimini."

"A pretty trifle," observed the erudite clergyman, "and undoubtedly, as suggested, a vial of old perfume. What strange meaning would it have carried to our friend, could he have lived to receive it?"

But something was stirring feebly in the mind of Mr. Joseph Spence, and for some time he stood with knitted brows. What was it that his friend had whispered about Bimini? There was an island . . . and a poem . . .

His eyes came back to the gray face on the pillow, and his grief burst from him afresh.

"I shall never part with it," he sobbed. "It shall be buried with me!"

CHAPTER NINE

IN WHICH THERE ARE QUEER HAPPENINGS AT AN INN

Oh, some that's good and godly ones they say that it's a sin
To troll the jolly bowl around, and let the dollars spin;
But I'm for toleration, and for drinking at an inn,
   Says the old bold mate of Henry Morgan.
                    —JOHN MASEFIELD.

Toward the beginning of the end of that violent century in which we have been adventuring, that saw the calm passing of Mr. Pope and the tardy arrival of the vial at his bedside, certain strange matters befell in one of England's seaports, which contribute not a little to our entertaining and curious history, already so rich in piety and wisdom.

Near the docks of this maritime village stood a tavern of wide popularity, before the door of which, in gusty weather, a miniature windmill tossed its arms, at once to advertise the tavern's name and, after a fashion, the brisk nature of its trade and entertainment. A bright and comforting little place it must have been on many a night of storm and blackness, when the fire roared within and the tempest roared without; such a place as one often finds in the forefront of romantic novels. The sign was newly painted; the windows had neat red curtains; the floor was cleanly sanded; and over all presided that most genial of hosts, John England, and the aging negress who was his lawful wife.

On either side of the tavern there was a street, and there were doors that opened conveniently on both, a circumstance that made it possible to see the occupants of the low room, in spite of the clouds of tobacco smoke that hung always above it. Thus it was plainly to be seen that the customers were mostly seafaring men, with here and there— like tropic birds in a northern aviary—the red coat of a soldier from the neighbouring barracks. They talked loudly and with emphatic gestures, as they drank the health of the King's Majesty; wine, horses, and politics were discussed with authority by experts in varying stages of liquor. They spoke boldly and without fear of successful contradiction. At times they viewed with alarm. Upon a desolate evening in early winter, they argued with such eloquence that a small man, hanging nervously about the front door, was almost afraid to enter. In the end, however, finding himself unobserved, he adjusted his seedy cuffs and sauntered in, seating himself in a remote corner out of eyeshot of the majority. Whatever his fears might have been, they had been needless. Only the landlord paid him the slightest attention.

This landlord, who was somewhat past his seventieth year, seemed rather to enjoy than to discourage the uproar. There was something fine and hearty about the old fellow that inspired instant confidence. It was whispered that, in his youth, John England had been a pirate, and that even now his mattress was stuffed with the whiskers of the men that he had slain; but there were few who took stock in so palpable a libel. The benevolence of his countenance, the piety of his utterance, and the fringe of white hair that lay like a halo upon his head, were in themselves enough to discourage the report. He had been a tall man in his prime, and was still vigorous in spite of his obvious disabilities. His left leg was cut off close by the hip, and under his left shoulder he carried a crutch, which he managed with wonderful dexterity, hopping about upon it like a bird. His face, of the colour of beef suet, was broad and ham-shaped, and was set with small eyes of an indistinguishable hue, beneath which lay always the merriest of smiles. Indeed, he seemed to be in the most cheerful of spirits as he moved, whistling, among the tables, with a cheery word or a slap on the shoulder for the more favoured of his guests. "Long John," his friends called him, and they said it lovingly, as men speak of their dogs and horses.

In time, and seemingly by chance, he came upon the little man who had slipped in out of the darkness. Thereupon, his small eyes became even smaller, so that they shone in the great face like crumbs of glass, and, slapping his guest boisterously on the knee, he contrived at the same instant to strike the man's ankle sharply with the steel point of his crutch. The little man cried out in agony.

"Hush up, you fool!" grated John England. "That's to teach you a little caution. Have you lost your wits, you numbskull? What brings you here at this hour o' night?"

"There is—there is another one," stammered the little man nervously, clutching at his ankle. "I came to tell you, there is another——"

Again the crutch struck smartly against his shinbone, and with difficulty he restrained his shout of pain.

"Say it again, will you, you swab?" cried England, in a furious undertone. "D'ye want the whole room to hear you? Get out of my inn, you lubber,

and wait in the proper place." With sudden suspicion, he asked: "Where is it?"

The little man was still nursing his ankle. "In
the cart," he answered ruefully, "in the stable.
You needn't be so free with that stick o' yourn,
John. I ain't your nigger."

"Be thankful I don't lay it around your ears,"
said the landlord, with a savage smile. "Get back
to the stable, and cover it with straw, since it's
there. And after this, keep out o' sight till I've
closed the shop, you swipe!"

He laughed heartily and slapped the other's knee
again.

"That's a good one," he chuckled, for the entire
room to hear. "Well, good luck to you, shipmate,
and I'll see you when you get back."

The little man staggered, limping, into the night,
as the nearest drinkers looked up, and an instant
later his thin figure passed the steaming windows
of the inn and vanished in the darkness.

John England continued his peregrination
among the tables. He exchanged a word here and
a quip there, in his inimitable fashion. He beamed
impartially upon all and sundry who had paid their
shot. He pinched an arm or a shoulder with im-
perturbable good humour. In the centre of the
room a tall soldier was entertaining a group of

pop-eyed seamen, who were paying for his grog.
By an extraordinary freak of nature, calculated to
help him through life, he had been born without
gums and teeth, and could so manipulate his nose
and chin as to take up a piece of money from the
table between them. Indeed, he often made a considerable sum, of an evening, lifting silver pieces in
this fashion, and transferring them to his pocket.
To effect the transfer to the pocket, however, it
was necessary to employ a hand; and the accomplished performer at all times preferred silver to
copper. Upon solicitation, he would also contract
his face suddenly and put his nose inside his mouth,
thus bringing his lips nearly to a level with his
forehead. He grinned hideously as England approached, and in his toothless rumble suggested
that he would like to show the boys a trick with a
glass of gin.

"And so you shall," cried Long John heartily.
"A glass of hot gin for Mr. Baker, Jamaica!" he
called, and the negress brought it to them.

The glass was set down upon a table, near the
edge, and the soldier bent above it. He chivvied
it to the edge with his nose, so that the base of the
glass hung partly over, then seizing it between
his nose and chin, bore it triumphantly around the
room.

A rapturous thumping of tankards greeted this astonishing performance, and there were cheers for "good old Baker." One might have supposed the feat to have been performed that evening for the first time. The uproar, however, merely expressed the immemorial readiness of citizens with tankards to cheer for anybody at the proper hour of the evening. Returning to his own table, Private Baker tossed off the gin and reseated himself among his friends.

In a corner arose a sudden babble of voices. Another redcoat was upon his feet haranguing his listeners upon the subject of the American rebels. A seaman who had traded with these irritating people, had dared to speak well of them; even to uphold their summary disposition of certain packages of tea, thrown overboard in Boston Harbour. The seaman protested feebly. "I'll leave it to Long John!" he said, as the peg-leg stumped into their midst.

John England considered profoundly, resting easily upon his crutch.

"Well, lads," he answered, at length, "as a fair man, I won't say as there isn't justice on *both* sides, for, mind you, I've lived among those very people, myself. They're our cousins, if it comes to that. But this matter o' the tea, now, is something very differ-

ent, something very, very different. It depends, you
see, upon the *sperrit* in which the deed was done.
If 'twas to defy King George—God bless him!—
why, then, says I, 'twas very wrong; ay, very
wrong indeed. But if 'twas to mannyfest their disapproval o' *tea*—then, by the powers, I'm with
them! 'Tis a dreadful habit to fall into, lads, and
you may lay to that. For myself, I prefers *rum!*"

A roar of laughter went up from the crowded
room, and England chuckled. But a high, cold
voice struck across the chamber, charged with the
quality of a knife gleam.

"Very well spoken, Mr. England," said the
voice, "and your sentiments do you credit. It is,
however, neither the hour nor the place, perhaps,
for a final disposition of the political situation.
That may be safely left, I imagine, to His Majesty's
ministers."

A tall young officer, wrapped to his throat in a
military cape, stood in the far doorway, surveying
the scene with keen, derisive eyes. A murmur ran
around the walls, and the redcoats began to rise
quickly in all parts of the chamber.

"It's Captain André," muttered one of the soldiers. "He's a terror for roundin' us up, after
hours. There'll be extra duty for this!"

But Long John hobbled forward with suave

humility. "Your sarvant, Cap'n," he said, with a jerk. "A bit of a discussion that I thought 'twas as well to nip in the bud, so to speak."

The officer bowed sardonically, and again his voice cut the dense atmosphere of the room. "To your quarters, men!"

They saluted sharply and filed before him through the doorway. The captain paused on the threshold. After a moment, he beckoned the landlord to his side. They stood together, facing the darkness.

"England," said the captain, in crisp, even tones, "you have a great influence over these men. You wear your country's name, however you came by it. It may or may not be your own; I have heard that it is not. I trust, at any rate, that you wear also your country's honour. I cannot control the tongues of my men when they have passed beyond my hearing, nor the tongues of your seamen; but it is my opinion that soldiers should not hold opinions. It is possible that among your customers there may be agents of the colonies. I look to you to preserve here, at least, the comparative decorum of a barroom, and to see that political discussion of a dangerous nature is discouraged."

The landlord laid two fingers against his brow in salute.

"I'll do it, Cap'n. Trust me for that. You honour me by your confidence. I can handle them without offense, sir. They look up to me as to a mother, bless their hearts! *Lambs* ain't the word for 'em when I say the word. I began this as a law-abidin' place, an' law-abidin' it will stay."

"Very good," said the captain, and with a brief nod he followed his men into the street.

John England returned to his own chair in the little room that opened off the bar, where he exchanged a few words with the negress. When half an hour had passed, he rose nimbly to his single foot, and with his wife's assistance struggled into a stout jacket. Then, knotting a scarf about his throat and pulling a seaman's cap low upon his head, he left the tavern by a rear door. The passage into which he emerged was long and narrow, and was filled with a thin cold rain and a piercing wind. He proceeded along its length to the street and stumped across into an alley, where he paused before the gaunt stable that appertained to the Windmill Tavern.

At his low whistle, a door was opened, and a dim light fell outward and illumined his person. He entered and closed the door behind him. Two men were in the stable, the small, ferret-faced man whom he had driven from the inn, and another.

The little man resumed his seat upon an upturned barrow, and with red eyes looked sullenly at the newcomer. The second man lay at full length upon his back, with closed eyelids. His garments were stained and damp and much too large for him. He was dead. He lay upon a bed of straw spread for him in a small cart, and the lean horse that had conveyed him stood shivering, with hanging head.

For a moment, the Windmill's landlord was silent, regarding the dead man's face. The little man on the barrow whistled nervously. After a moment he interrupted his melody and spat venomously into a corner.

"Quite a young fellow, I should say," observed Long John, at length. "No more than twenty, would be my own guess. How did he die, if I might be so bold as to ask?" He eyed his companion with whimsical shrewdness.

The little man shrugged. "How should *I* know?" he demanded. "Better for him if he was older. The young ones pay the best."

"So they do, so they do," agreed the one-legged man, with great good humour. "As true a word as ever was spoken, Tom Lewis. You ain't as sociable as usual, it seems to me. Thinking, belike, o' the tap I give you with this old stick, eh? Well, 'twas for your good, me lad. Youth is that reckless, and lacks caution. It never stops to think. Bless me, I were the same at your age. Always into everything, without a second thought, and like as not without a first. Not that I couldn't do with a little o' that same youth! 'Tis a brave gift, I will admit. Yet see what it has brought this unfortunate young man to. Pore young chap! Like as not he had a sweetheart, and there he lies! He was young—and so he died."

"He was not knifed," snapped the small man angrily. "He died natural, an' was buried on Monday. He was a young man from the University."

"Dear, dear! From the University! A young man of eddication! He knew Latin and Greek, maybe, and could read the stars. And there he lies. There's fate in this, Tom Lewis. A queer thing is life, indeed! For, look you, by his death he passes from one institootion of learning to another, an' what he didn't learn hisself, others'll learn now from him. A very profound thought. Ah, a queer thing is life!" Long John sighed deeply. After a moment, he smiled. "Well, well, here's your money then, Tom; and good luck to you. Four shillings extra, because he's young, and another because he's eddicated and to pay for your crack on the ankle. No one can say that I ain't generous with them as helps me."

The other got to his feet with alacrity. "Now, that's handsome of you, John," he acknowledged. "Damned if it isn't! As for the crack on the ankle, 'twas my own fault. If so be it that you wanted me to, now, I could stop in at the doctor's and let drop a hint, maybe, that you've something for him, eh?"

The landlord shook his head. "I'll see to that, myself," he said. "Like as not you'd go blundering in an' tell him about it in front of his family, or one of his patients. Then where'd his business be, and mine, too? You run along on your own and forget about this. It's your job to get 'em and mine to sell 'em, and a very fair arrangement, too." His smile suddenly vanished, and he added: "And look to it that you keep your clapper quiet about what you know, or I shouldn't be surprised if you'd bring a nice penny yourself, one o' these days. Fresh corpses is scarce among the medical perfession, and they ain't any too p'tic'lar where they get 'em."

"I ain't a fool," said the red-eyed man, climbing upon the wheel. "Give me a lift now, John, and let's get it over."

He scrambled into the cart and, treading in the loose straw, kicked against a small object that lay concealed there. The thing gleamed for an instant.

and tinkled along the boards. The innkeeper's ears pricked upward. "What's that?" he asked, and snatched at it, at the same instant that the other bent forward. The small man came up with only a handful of straw.

"What's this?" cried England sharply, and carried the gleaming object to the light. "By the powers, Tom Lewis, what've you been up to, now? Gold, as I'm a living sinner, and diamonds into the bargain! So you've added burglary to your other accomplishments! It weren't enough to put your neck in danger with body-snatching!"

"It's mine," said the ghoul sullenly. "Give it back!"

"Give it back, is it? It's yours! An heirloom, perhaps, or a pretty gift from a lady!"

With eyes that were glistening pinpoints in his head, the landlord examined the slender vial that he had captured in the straw. "What's this?" he cried again exultantly, and held it closer to the light. "There's writin' on this bottle, Tom Lewis. Your hand of write, perhaps? Addressed to the lady of your choice, belike? Why, you murdering villain, it's French!" He looked swiftly into the face of the dead man.

"It wasn't—his," said the body snatcher. "He died natural, I tell you. I—I found it."

"L-low de Bimini," read England slowly. "Lumme, if it isn't! *Bimini!* Why, 'tis an island in the Indies. Many's the time I've passed it in the old days. And 'low' means water. Why, 'tis a little old smelling bottle, Tom Lewis. Some Frenchman's given it a name. Dear, dear, now! All wrapped in gold and with these pretty diamonds, too!" His face was creased and seamed with an hundred pleasant wrinkles.

Suddenly, he turned upon his companion. "Well, Tom, what about it?"

"I found it, I tell you," insisted the resurrectionist; and as the landlord's eyes narrowed and the landlord's brows approached each other in a formidable manner, he added: "I found it in the grave."

"In the grave! Come now, Tom, there's no secrets between you and old John. Let's have the truth, the whole truth, and nothing but the truth."

"I told you the truth. I found it in the grave of this—this—gentleman. I don't know how it got there. 'Twas buried with him, I suppose. A trinket that he wanted to keep alongside o' him. Why shouldn't he?"

"Why *shouldn't* he!" roared John England, swiftly shifting his ground. "He *should*, and he *did!* The question is, me lad, what right had you to remove it?" He shook his head reproachfully. "It ain't lucky, Tom Lewis," he said. "No good'll come o' this. Robbing the dead is a bad business, me lad, I wouldn't be in your shoes for a lot, I'll tell you straight. 'Tis different about the pore creetur, hisself. Being dead, he has no use for his body, an' 'tis only right that it should serve the ends o' science. But this little bottle, now, is different. You've committed a sacrilege, Tom Lewis, that's what you've done, and I'm ashamed to know you."

The body snatcher grinned evilly. "I'll take the chance," he said. "It ain't on *your* conscience."

"Ain't it, though?" demanded England. "An' whose conscience is it on, if it ain't on mine? Who hired you to get this pore fellow out of his grave on a cold night and bring him here to lie in my stable? Who'd swing in chains if he was found here in my straw? I'll tell you it's on my conscience, too, and I'm mighty uneasy about it."

"Give it to *me*, then, and I'll put it back," suggested the other. "The harm ain't done yet."

"Ah, but it is," sighed the Windmill's landlord. "The harm was done when you took it out, Tom. Like as not if you tried to put it back, you'd only be caught, an' then what good would be accomplished? No, 'tis bad enough as it is, and we must make the best of it. I'll take this little bottle, myself, and that'll take it off *your* soul; and I'll give it to Jamaica, who's only a nigger, and that'll take it off *my* soul." He wiped his brow with a big red handkerchief and seemed deeply relieved by this solution of the problem. " 'Twas lucky I thought o' that," he added, "or I don't know what'd have become of both of us."

For a moment his associate seemed about to spring; then swallowing his wrath, he asked: "What d'ye s'pose it's worth?"

"Not a penny over a pound," answered Long John promptly. "The diamonds don't look like real diamonds, to me, and anyway they're pretty small. You can see for yourself that the gold is pretty old and getting thin."

"Then give me a pound for it, and it's yours."

"I'll do it!" swore John England. "You've done me some good turns in your time, Tom Lewis, and I'll give you the pound for old time's sake. There you are, and the bottle's mine. I'll give it to Jamaica in the morning. What were his name, the pore young man?"

"Wishart," said the body snatcher. "And the bottle wasn't exactly in *his* grave. 'Twas in the grave next to him. We sort o' broke through, when

we was getting him out. 'Twas an accident—an'
that's all I know," he concluded with an oath.
"Now, perhaps, you'll give me a lift. I'd like to
get out o' here by daylight."

After all, reflected Lewis, as he drove away, a
pound was a pound, and he would probably have
got no more for the bottle from a dealer. John
England, when he attempted to sell it, might get
even less. It was to be hoped so, at any rate. He
whistled cheerily, and whipping up his sorry animal, disappeared in the rain and from the high
history of the vial.

John England, when he had made all snug,
returned to the privacy of his little cabin, as he
called his room under the staircase at the Windmill. He sat late into the night examining his prize.
That it was very old, was certain. Older even than
the last century. He turned it lovingly in his hands.
Ah, the dear gold! The sweet diamonds! Why, it
might be worth—anything! The red wax,
slightly crumbling, at the mouth, puzzled him.
Why should anyone have troubled to seal the vial?
Then a thought occurred to him. It *might* contain
poison. Those old vials often did. Many a tale of
poison vials had he heard from the old Spaniards,
in the days when he had sailed the Indies. The
unknown Frenchman, no doubt, had himself sailed

the main in that day. How else could he have heard of Bimini?

Long John reached for his crutch and stood upright. He removed a cloth that hung over a wire cage, and spoke to a red and gold parrot within. Then he opened the wire door, and the parrot flew out with a squawk and perched upon his shoulder.

"Well, Cap'n, what d'ye think o' that?" asked England, and he scratched the parrot's head with the gleaming vial. "Reminds you a bit o' the old times, eh?"

"Pieces of eight, pieces of eight, pieces of eight!" cried the parrot, with great rapidity.

"Well, no," said England, with his crinkly smile, "it ain't exactly pieces of eight yet, Cap'n; but we'll turn it into 'em before long."

He returned the bird to its cage and replaced the cloth, whereupon it instantly subsided.

Yes, the vial *might* contain poison. He must look into this matter. Tom Lewis had said too much or not enough. He polished the vial tenderly and hid it away in a cabinet upon his wall, beside the other trophies left to him of his career—a crumpled parchment map, a curved horn of powder, and a handsomely chased pistol of Spanish workmanship.

A fortnight later, there was an alarm at the inn,

and at an unholy hour. The place had been closed for more than forty minutes, when the heavy knock resounded through the house. England slowly raised himself and listened. But whoever the disturber was, he had no intention of going away. The landlord tiptoed to the door. From the voices beyond, apparently three men stood without.

"What d'ye want?" roared Long John through the panels.

"Open the door, England," replied a high, cold voice, which he recognized as Captain André's. "I want to talk to you."

The door was slowly opened. On the doorstep loomed the tall figure of the young officer, and two others stood behind him on the walk. The captain pushed past and into the room.

"Get a light, England," he ordered sharply.

"Right away, Cap'n—certainlee!" answered Long John. "Coming right away, sir!" He hobbled out of the room and came back presently with a light. "Might I make so bold as to ask you what the trouble may be, Cap'n?"

"The trouble is Tom Redfield and two others," said André briefly. "They are believed to have deserted and to be hiding somewhere along the wharves."

"Not here, sir!" cried England.

"Perhaps not," said the captain, "but it is our duty to search."

"Quite right, sir, and I'll go with you and hold the light. But you'll see I'm right, sir. Nary hide nor hair of any of 'em have I seen. They'd know better than to ask old John to help 'em desert. Yes, sirree!"

"I hope so," was the captain's reply; and, calling to his men, he began a search of the premises that ended as John England had predicted.

"And now, gentlemen," said the landlord hospitably, "a bit of hot rum to guard against the weather. A raw cold night it is, and no mistake."

The captain smiled. "Very well," he agreed. "I really can't think of any reason why I shouldn't, and so I shall. Give the men a ration, and let's sit down."

"Right into my own little cabin, sir," begged the host. "Not many has ever seen it, but it'll be honoured by your presence, sir."

He led the way into his private room, after the soldiers had been seated elsewhere, then hurried off after his fiery liquor. On the old table used by the landlord as a desk, the captain saw with surprise an object that filled him with delight. It was a gleaming golden vial enclosed in lighter bands of gold and adorned with a dozen or more of flashing gems. He picked it up and read the inscription on one of the bands. Then he read it again—and again. An expression of amazement crossed his face, and a low whistle sprang out of his puckered lips. He looked quickly around the room and back again at the glistening vial.

This England! Who was he? Queer stories had been whispered about him when he had come up out of nobody knew where, to purchase the old tavern from the widow of its late proprietor. His name was the name of a celebrated pirate, long dead; his wife was a West Indian negress.

Bimini ! It was more than conceivable that this man had visited the island. But the fountain legend was long exploded. For two hundred and fifty years, *that* ghost had been laid. Why, then, these "waters of Bimini"? Was it a commercialization of the name? A hoax? Or a—survival? The thing—the vial—was perhaps centuries old. And if this man had been a pirate—had ravaged the Spanish Main, in his youth—had plundered shrines and cathedrals!

Captain André drew a long breath. The inscription, however, should be in Spanish.

He looked up. Long John was entering the cabin with a tray of glasses. The glance of the Windmill's landlord fell upon the captain and his occupation, and the beadlike eyes gleamed with swift suspicion. Then the great face smiled.

"I see, sir, that you've found my little antike! A very pretty bit it is, sir, if I say it as shouldn't. Ah, the eyes don't ache that saw that bottle first, sir."

"I should imagine not," said Captain André. "It is very pretty, as you say. If it is not an impertinent question, where did you come by it, England?"

"Bless your heart," cried Long John, "there ain't no secret about it. I had it of a seaman who was down on his luck, pore chap, and I bought it off him. That was a long time ago, sir, nigh on to fifty years. Five pounds is what I gave him, and it's worth a lot more now, I shouldn't be surprised."

"You have never opened it?" asked the captain.

"Not I, sir! 'Cause why? Well, I'll be honest with you. I didn't know whether 'twere perfume or poison, sir, and that's a fact."

The captain raised his steaming glass. "Success to you, Mr. England," he nodded. "The vial interests me a great deal. I have a passion for things that are old, when they are also charming. You would not consider selling it, I suppose?"

"Well, now, sir, it hadn't exactly occurred to me, and that's a fact. I've took quite a fancy to it, in all these years, as mayhap you'll understand, sir."

"Quite so! Well, it's a pity, for I am really quite delighted with it. I should have been willing to pay you double what you gave for it. There is a lady who would value it highly. But, no matter."

He finished his glass and stood up. "By the way, England, there is said to be a great deal of very good brandy to be purchased hereabouts, which has somehow got upon the market without the usual custom-house entries and certificates. One suspects that it comes from France, and in a swift brig. I trust that *you* will not be embarrassed by any investigation into the matter."

He picked up the vial again, without looking at the landlord's face, and smiled happily. "A very delightful thing," he said again. "I am genuinely sorry that it is not for sale. Should you ever change your mind, consider me as a possible purchaser."

He started for the door. John England spoke quickly.

"Well, now, Cap'n, since your heart is so set on that bit o' gold and glass, I don't know why I should hang on to it like it was a splinter o' the true Cross. Jest you take it along with you, sir, with the compliments of old John. And very glad for you to have it, sir."

The captain smiled. "I'm afraid that won't do at all, John," he said affably. "One can't accept gifts in that fashion, you know. It isn't done. But I've offered to purchase the trifle, and I will. Here is your ten pounds, and the sale is consummated. And many thanks for your toddy. Good-night!"

The door closed behind him. For a moment, John England stood where he had stopped, bending slightly forward, his hand upon the door, upon his face an odd and indescribable expression, in which were blended fear and hatred and admiration.

John André, hurrying through the night, his cloak buttoned tightly about him, one hand holding his sword clear of his legs, the other clutching at his hat that the wind momently threatened to remove, felt the vial against his breast, under his jacket, and smiled the smile of one who has driven a shrewd bargain. He felt no shame at having coerced England, who was no better than he should be; and he was distinctly curious about the vial. That it contained the veritable waters of the lost fountain of youth was, of course, beyond human credence. Attractive as was the thought, he put it from him. Time and again he put it from him. . . . And ever it came back to torture and inflame him.

"Nonsense!" He spoke aloud in the darkness, and his men, tramping behind him, hastened forward to await his orders. He sent them back to their positions.

It was madness, of course. A very happy accident, this episode that had brought him so attractive a trinket; but no miracle. The age of miracles was past. The vial, however, was charming, and would make a delicious gift for Lucasta. He would write a poem to accompany it, in which he would set forth the folly of presenting vivid youth to one already possessed of it in such abundance; and thereafter she might daub the water on her dress and handkerchief. They would laugh together at the legend, and pretending to believe it, each would sip gaily from the vial's lip and call himself immortal.

> Lucasta, though thy locks of gold
> Such wealth of Spanish treasure cries,
> Bid him who comes with tread o'er bold . . .

It would be a very pretty thing indeed!

In the morning, the captain's world fell to pieces. Within the same hour, he heard the tidings of the lady's elopement with a naval officer of ill repute and received the order that was to send him overseas to the rebellious colonies.

In the bag that held his rings and buckles, went the vial of Ortubia, back to the Americas.

CHAPTER TEN

IN WHICH AN AUTHOR AND HIS CHARACTER ARE WELL MET

Ill-fated and mysterious man !—bewildered in the bril-
liancy of thine own imagination, and fallen in the flames
of thine own youth ! Again in fancy I behold thee !
—E. A. POE.

Three quarters of a century after the momentous events just narrated, the steam packet from Richmond set down upon the docks at Baltimore a small, dark man of shabby-genteel appearance, who glanced quickly about him, as if expecting recognition, then strode briskly into the city. Afternoon was waning, and over the sky was spreading a dark threat of storm. In the shops, the proprietors were beginning to light their lamps. Presently, a thin rain began to fall, and the traveller hastened his steps toward shelter. Despite the bleakness of the occasion, a high humour perched jauntily upon him; an unwonted humour that he wore at the rakish angle of a new hat. His stick tapped the boards with arrogant challenge; his restless eyes gleamed with a sardonic mirth. So arresting was the hauteur of his cameolike features that a passing woman stopped to look back and admire. Sensing her admiration, he paused before the window of a small shop and ostentatiously adjusted his stock before resuming his march.

At the intersection of two thoroughfares, under the canopy of a cheap hotel, he halted and stared around him at the bustling life in the streets; at the homing throngs that passed him in either direction. For a moment his heart sank. *Face on face in the city—would never the faces end?* There was at least a poem in the situation. *Face on face in the city—and never the face of a friend!* A wave of self-pity overwhelmed him and passed slowly. After a time, he smiled. This was the city of his youth. How he had loathed and loved it! For twenty years, it had been whispered, no friend had seen this man smile; but upon this gray day he smiled again, and, smiling, jingled in his pocket the few silver pieces that remained to him. This was an occasion of holiday. The follies of youth were long behind him. Ahead, a new and glittering chapter was opening its pages. He peered into the future, and suddenly life seemed almost bewilderingly bright. What of the paltry dollars in his pocket? At a single blow, perhaps, he would recoup his fallen fortunes and live forever at his ease.

Only one episode must be allowed to intervene—dinner! The boat journey had been long and chilling. Dinner—and a bottle of wine!

He looked dubiously at the garish entrance to the hostelry, and mentally calculated the sum of money in his pocket. Then, with firm step and smiling eye, he entered the place.

At the cashier's rostrum, in the dining room, sat an ageing spinster, watching the diners with listless gaze. She was almost offensively plain. Her straight teeth projected from her mouth as if driven forth by the violence of her shrill tongue. She was lank, dry, and yellow. Ten years dropped from her shoulders as he bowed, and twenty as, with his air of commanding diffidence, he wished her good-evening. Her eyes followed him with a wild hope as he sought a corner table and melted into the deepening shadows.

An ancient darky shambled forward and cried out in surprise. "Lord-a-marcy, Massa Poe! Am dat you?"

The sombre poet, thus revealed, smiled wryly. "You are a clever rascal, Jeff," he replied. "In the entire city, you are the first to recognize and welcome me. I shall admit the indictment on one condition only: that you bring me instantly a bottle and a glass. Need I say more?"

Widely grinning, the black servitor departed upon his errand. The poet, waiting for his wine, drummed restlessly upon the table. A wax taper gleamed before him, and upon this he fixed his melancholy gaze. After a moment, while the spinster gasped at her desk, he leaned forward and, removing it from its holder, pinched out the flame. Then, quietly, he transferred the candle to his pocket and again leaned back in his chair.

"Another taper, Jeff," he said, when the bottle had been placed before him; and when it had been brought, he filled his glass and held it to the light. For an instant, he hesitated, then raised the glass to his lips and drained it at a draught.

" 'Fo' God, Massa Poe," observed the astonished Negro, "yo' cert'nly swallered dat licker powerful quick!"

"It is to celebrate my swearing-off," said the poet solemnly, and he filled his glass again. "To-morrow, I shall be done with it forever." Again he tilted the liquid to his lips, and shuddered when he set down the glass.

On the other side of the dining room, a man arose and came forward. He was a tall man, in immaculate linen garments, which gave him somewhat the appearance of a Singhalese planter. A great diamond blazed on one of his fingers.

Under a glossy black moustache, his white teeth gleamed like the denture of a piano keyboard. Immediately, there was an outcry.

"Poe!" exclaimed the tall man delightedly.

"Legrand!" cried the poet, springing to his feet.

They shook hands heartily, while the diners stared and raised their brows.

"This *is* a surprise," said the man called Legrand. "I thought you were in Richmond."

"I am in Aberystwyth, as you perceive," retorted the sardonic poet. "But how fortuitous a meeting! You are the very man I have been wishing to see. Have you dined?"

"I was about to order when I saw you. You will join me, I hope?"

"I was about to extend the same invitation. Do sit down. I have a fascinating story for you. Quite in your line, you know. Buried treasure, and all that sort of thing."

"Good God!" said Legrand. "Again?"

They seated themselves at the poet's table. "Does it concern the lady behind the cage?" continued Legrand, with a smile. "She is eyeing us with a somewhat proprietary air."

The poet was not deeply flattered. He was aware of the fatal effect he had upon women of whatever age and station. Such things were always happening. Was it his fault that his black hair lay in curls upon his high, white forehead? That his eyes were of tragic brilliance above his well-turned nose and neat black moustache? He shrugged and bent his head over the pencilled card of dinner dishes. For a moment, he looked anxiously at the right-hand column for the enlightening figures there displayed. Had he accepted Legrand's invitation, or had Legrand accepted *his*? At length, he ordered, and lay back luxuriously in his chair.

It was a pleasant place, he reflected, this large dining room with its little gleaming tapers and dark-shadowed corners. Not at all the sort of place in which he ordinarily appeased his hunger.

Legrand, when the order had been given, watched him for a time in silence. Poe felt his companion's gaze and knew the thoughts that were passing in his mind. Neatly, even nattily dressed, as he was, the poet realized that there must be about him the unconcealable hints of poverty so long associated with his name. He resented the silent sympathy.

"My dear fellow," said Legrand, at last, "I can't tell you how glad I am to see you. We hear a great deal about you, these days. You are becoming quite famous."

The melancholy poet again drained his glass

before replying. "And infamous," he added, shrugging. "It is all the same, you know. Let them but shout loudly enough, and I care not what they say."

"But what a cynic!" continued the other. "I should have thought that by this time you would be quite—what is the phrase?—'o'erswol'n with pride.'"

"Not a stiver of it," asserted Poe. "Believe me, Legrand, I have too few friends worthy of the name, to wish to forget any of them. My pride is reserved for the mounting number of my foes. In youth, you know, we hope to succeed to please those whom we love; in age, to spite those whom we hate." He laughed lightly. "My ill luck in making enemies has been little short of phenomenal. Fortunately, they have all written books."

His friend laughed also. "I suspect, however, that you have just stated the reason why you enjoy such enmity," he ventured.

"Ha!" cried the poet. "So you, too, read my reviews! Well, it is true. They like me not at all, these little essayists and poetasters. And so, like sheep, they foregather and trample me."

"I trust it has not spoiled your appetite for grilled kidneys?"

"It has not," declared Poe, with decision; and

he turned eagerly to the steaming plate that the old Negro set before him.

Legrand raised his brows inquiringly. "A bottle of wine to celebrate your return?" he asked. "I note that you have not sworn off."

The black waiter paused uncertainly, and the poet made an eloquent gesture. "A bottle of wine, Jeff," he ordered, "to celebrate my return. And some cheroots, too."

They attacked their kidneys with gusto, nodding brightly at each other from time to time.

"By the way, Poe," said Legrand suddenly, "did you know that the words *abstemious* and *facetious* contain all the vowels in their consecutive order?"

The poet laughed. "It's true, isn't it? What genius discovered that, I wonder?"

"I saw it stated in a newspaper the other day, with other useful and informing items. I am interested in the curiosities of the alphabet, you may remember."

"I remember it very well," said Poe seriously. "The fact is, Legrand, I have been thinking about your talents in that direction for some hours."

At this point, the Negro returned with the bottle of wine, and for a time conversation languished.

Legrand, as he watched an entire tumbler of the liquor disappearing down his friend's throat, appeared as astonished as the black waiter had been.

"Hold on, Poe!" he cried humorously. "That's no way to drink wine."

The poet leaned back in his chair. He smiled gently and half closed his eyes. For some minutes, he puffed languidly at his cheroot and watched the smoke rings float away into the mysterious shadows. Save for the glimmering tapers, the room was almost without light. The lamps burned but feebly. Outside, the rain was falling more heavily. Poe's tragic eyes were fixed upon the taper before him. At length he spoke in a dreamy undertone.

"Wax tapers, Legrand," he said in his melodious voice. "How usual, and yet how lovely! We think of them, when we think of them at all, as commonplaces. Yet they are the veritable flambeaux of faëry. A white metamorphosis from the flowers, crowned with the most intangible of all visible mysteries."

"Charming!" cried his companion. "Why, one might make a poem of it, Poe."

The poet gestured gracefully. "One shall," he murmured. "Yes, I shall do it to-night, and send it off to Graham, to-morrow."

He reached for the wine bottle and found it